Other books by Kathryn Quick:

Stealing April's Heart
Jessie's Wedding
Blue Diamond

FALLING
FOR YOU

FALLING FOR YOU

·

Kathryn Quick

AVALON BOOKS
NEW YORK

PRINTED IN THE UNITED STATES OF AMERICA
ON ACID-FREE PAPER
BY HADDON CRAFTSMEN, BLOOMSBURG, PENNSYLVANIA

For Mom

Thanks to the New Jersey Devils for the inspiration
and the DFC for support and the great times
at the games and on the road.

Chapter One

"Mom, are you all right?"

Through the fog beginning to clear inside her head, Stephanie Thomas recognized her son, Michael's, voice. Other things were coming into focus too; the cold, the wet, the pain in her ankle and the one at the back of her head. She cracked open her right eye just a smidgen. When the picture came into focus, she saw Mike looming over her, inverted, his forehead even with her chin.

"Mom, can . . . you . . . hear . . . me?" he said, spacing out the words evenly.

"I'm not deaf, just uncoordinated," Stephanie replied. She twirled her forefinger in a circle in the air. "Do me a favor, Mike, do a one-eighty. Looking at you upside down is making me dizzy."

"Are you hurt bad?" Mike asked, circling her.

"I don't think so."

"Can you get up?"

Stephanie rose to her elbows and a sharp pain shot up her right leg, coupled with another wave of nausea.

1

"Give me a minute," she said, laying back down and closing her eyes.

"Think anything is broken?"

Stephanie flexed her fingers and moved her ankles from side to side. "Everything seems to be attached."

"So you're okay, right?"

"Basically."

"Good, then let's go. A crowd is gathering. Family time is over. Let's get out of here before some of the guys show up."

Stephanie opened both eyes and turned her aching head to the right. Eye level with a few dozen pairs of ice skates, she followed the white laces of one pair up to the face of another adolescent. He couldn't have been much older than her son, but he wore a jacket with the words SKATE GUARD emblazoned across the front.

"You okay, lady?" he asked.

"She's fine," Mike answered for her. He bent down and pulled on her arm, dragging her to a sitting position. "Mom, get up now," he pleaded.

The sudden change in position made Stephanie's head swim. Refusing to give in, she willed the ice rink to stop spinning around her like an Olympic skater going for a perfect ten, and put one hand onto the ice to steady herself before leaning against the wooden half-wall with Plexiglas on top that enclosed the rink.

"He's right. I'm fine."

She tried to stand, but the skate guard stopped her with a hand to her shoulder. "Don't move. I hafta get some help and call the owner."

"No," Mike protested. "You heard her, she said she's fine. You don't need to call anyone. She does stuff like this all the time. She tried to ski once." He tugged his mother's arm a few times, but she did not move. "She managed to get to a tree about a quarter of the way down the slope and held on to it until the ski patrol sent someone up to get her."

"The slope was pitched at this steep angle—" Stephanie started to explain, but Mike cut her off again with a nasty stare.

"Listen," the skate guard said, "if I don't follow procedure, it's my backside that will be skidding down a slippery slope. The rules say I hafta call the owner when someone falls this hard." He then turned his attention back to Stephanie. "Dontcha know how to stop?"

"Stop?" Mike said in a voice tinged with pubescent sarcasm. "She doesn't even know how to go straight. She's never been on skates before."

"Then why was she going so fast?"

Mike shrugged.

"Shoulda took a lesson, lady," the skate guard said.

Stephanie glanced at the clock mounted on the wall across the way. Five minutes. That's the length of time she'd been on ice skates. Just long enough for her to lose more points with her son. She looked at him. He appeared mortified.

Her face burned with the heat of embarrassment as the voices around her grew louder. This was another fine mess she'd gotten herself into. Her sweatshirt was damp and getting clammy, her jeans were getting colder wherever the ice touched them, and she was sure she had what would be the beginning of frostbite. She didn't want anyone to fuss over her. She wanted to go home, or at the very least, melt into the ice. She tried to stand and another feeling of nausea swelled so she sat back down.

She squeezed her eyes shut and tried to melt into the ice. All things considered, it appeared to be another typical day gone wrong in the Thomas household.

A man in tennis shoes slid to a stop next to the skate guard. "Is she all right?"

"I think she whacked her ankle against the boards when she fell."

"Is she here with anyone?"

"Me."

Martin St. Claire turned to the source of voice. "Hey, Mike. What are you doing here? Your team doesn't have a game until Monday."

"She's my mom, Mr. St. Claire."

"Oh." The kid looked positively destroyed. "What happened?"

"She wanted to try skating. I wanted her to take a lesson first, but no, she had to do it her way. Now look." He pointed down at his mother, who was now lying back on the ice. "She looks like she's trying to make frozen snow angels."

"What happened?" Marty repeated. He saw the young man's mouth thin into a frown.

Mike shook his head. "Went down harder than Nancy Kerrigan." He saw Marty's forehead crease and answered the question before it was asked. "Nineteen-ninety-four Olympic recap on ESPN."

Marty nodded and turned his attention back to Stephanie. He dropped to one knee. "Can she tell us her name?"

"Probably. I think it's her ankle more than her head."

"Do you think she can sit up?"

Stephanie cracked open one eye. "Why don't you ask me? It's not polite to talk about someone in the third person when they're right in front of you. Well, sort of in front. More like straight down and to the left. And to answer your question, no. When I try to sit up, my ankle really hurts, so you'll have to come down here if you want to talk."

"Sorry." Marty took off his jacket and gently lifted her head before sliding it underneath. "I know you're uncomfortable, but you'll have to hang in there for a few minutes. The squad's been called and should be here soon."

"Sounds like you've had some practice at this," Stephanie said, turning her head toward him.

"More than you can guess. The insurance company has had to handle a few more claims projected lately and unless . . ." He stopped speaking when his gaze met hers, feeling as though someone had sprayed liquid nitrogen on him, freezing him to the spot. Her eyes were the palest shade of blue he had ever seen, the color reminding him of the offensive zone line in a hockey rink. He somehow tore his gaze away from those eyes with their fringe of dark lashes to focus on the woman owning them.

Looking at the bigger picture didn't help him much at all. His senses began to react as though on autopilot. Sight was the first into action, focusing on her dark auburn hair and the way it contrasted sharply with the grayish white ice beneath it, giving him an edgy, aware kind of feeling. The light scent of her perfume somehow cut through the cold and hit his nose like an opposing player charging the net.

"Unless what?" he heard her ask.

Hearing responded next, tuning into the rich timbre of her voice and masking all the normal sounds of the ice rink. Her pleasing tone resonated through him like the sound of a finely tuned violin string vibrating through the air.

"What I meant was that I'm usually not this . . ." Almost against his will, he touched her shoulder, his hand seeming to tingle as though he had come in contact with a low voltage wire. It had never happened before, but for some reason four of his five senses had all converged on this woman at once. ". . . this scattered and . . ." Any shred of reason he had left suddenly launched an attack of its own and the urge to kiss her hit him like a ninety mile per-hour slap shot hitting the back of the net. "Whoa," he muttered in reaction, "Five out of five and—"

"Do you ever actually finish a sentence?" he heard her say over the jolt of all his basic instincts firing at once.

Still amazed at his reaction to the woman lying at his feet, he removed his hand from her shoulder and looked at it briefly before looking back at her. "On occasion. I apologize. How do you feel?"

"Wet and cold," Stephanie said.

Marty reached for the blanket another rink employee had retrieved from an office. He shook it open and covered her.

"That's not what's wet and cold." She started to sit up.

"Stop trying to do that," he cautioned, a protective instinct causing him to touch her shoulder. "You could have a concussion and not even realize it." Warmth again flickered on his skin. He looked from his hand to her eyes and saw surprise. He wondered if she felt it too, and managed a half-smile.

Stephanie smiled back at him. "I suppose so. I do get a little sick to my stomach when I try to get up."

"All the more reason not to." He looked over his shoulder in response to the sound of the oversized rink door being pulled open. "The squad's here."

"Move aside," one of two EMTs called out, weaving through the skaters still on the ice. Marty stood and moved out of the way when one dropped a back brace onto the ice next to Stephanie. "Don't get up," he ordered. "What happened?"

"She fell," Mike volunteered.

The EMT fastened a cervical collar around Stephanie's neck. "Do you know your name?" one of the EMTs asked, shining a light first in one of her eyes and then the other.

"Of course I do. It's Stephanie Thomas."

"And what day is it?"

"Friday."

"So far, so good."

"I'm *fine*," Stephanie insisted as the EMT slid a backboard under her and strapped it around her. "I don't need to be trussed up like a Thanksgiving turkey. I just need to get home."

"Well, you can't go home. Not just yet," Marty cut in. "You need to get checked out." He felt his mouth kick up in a grin.

"What are you smiling at?" Stephanie asked when she noticed.

"I'm sorry, but you do look a little like Hannibal Lechter." He tried to suppress it, but the grin grew wider. He covered his mouth with his hand. A fall was no laughing matter even though, from past experience with the dozens of spills skaters had taken on the ice since the rink opened, it appeared as though Stephanie Thomas would probably be all right.

"Keep that up and I'll bite *your* face," she warned, noticing his losing attempt to keep from grinning.

"Miss Thomas, can you move your arms and legs? Any pain here or here?" the EMT examining her asked.

"Yes, first question, no, second. I'm fine," she insisted.

"You really can't make that determination," Marty chimed in. "You said yourself that you feel a little sick when you try to get up." '

"Could be the hot dog I had at the refreshment stand."

"Could be a lot of things."

"Whatever it is, I can take care of myself."

"I hope better than you can skate," Marty said with a decided spark of bravado in his voice.

"What are you, a comedian in the offseason?"

"No, nervous chitchat I suppose. Sorry," Marty conceded before stepping back but keeping his gaze on her face.

Cripes, this man-woman thing was giving him an itch he wanted to scratch. Any woman who could make him sit up and take notice in a situation like this could be dangerous. Interesting dangerous that was. Maybe even worth-checking-out-more-closely dangerous, especially since he hadn't reacted this strongly to any woman in years. But to read anything into all the eye contact and spunky bantering seemed out of place right now.

Stephanie blew out a long breath of air as Marty helped the EMT hoist her up onto a waiting stretcher. "Who are you anyway?" she asked him, "and why all the questions?"

"I'm Martin St. Claire. I own the place."

She studied his face as he walked alongside her. "Oh, right. The hockey player."

"Ex-hockey player," Marty corrected. "I'm retired."

"I should have recognized you. But looking at you from down on the ice, you look different than you do on the poster on the wall of my son's room."

Marty pointed to his lips. "No mouthpiece or cage across my face."

Stephanie laughed. "And you said I looked like Hannibal Lechter." He laughed, and this time, she liked the sound.

She studied him as he walked alongside the stretcher. Martin St. Claire. How many times had she heard that name from her son? A million, at least. At around five hundred thousand, she thought she conjured up a pretty good picture of what Martin St. Claire must look like. But *this* Martin St. Claire wasn't anything like she'd imagined; not as big, not as brooding. From the stories and descriptions, and the way her son talked about him, she had pictured a tough, thuggish jock with missing front teeth and a burly body. Instead, she was staring up at a six-foot toned and tapered hunk, with hair the color of a field of wheat, and a pair of dark spicy-brown eyes that looked like trouble to her.

There were many times she wouldn't have minded meeting an attractive man like him, but this wasn't one of them. She had a headache the size of Alaska, a condition much too distracting to have fully functioning female hormones kick in properly. She did, however, feel a jolt of something as a few wayward ones took notice when her gaze met Marty's incredible eyes as he loomed over her on the way out of the arena.

"Are you feeling dizzy or something?" Marty asked. "You look a little funny. You're not going to do something that requires a bucket, are you?"

"No," Stephanie assured. She must have been staring

at his face like some sort of crazy woman, but she could explain that away. She was obviously unhinged by the knot on her head and not in her right mind. She looked at his broad shoulders to avoid staring at his handsome face. "Sorry we had to meet like this. I've heard so much about you and your hockey career from my son. He has an autographed puck in a plastic protector on his dresser."

Mike elbowed his way to his mother's side. "Is she going to be all right?" he asked.

"We're not doctors," one of the EMTs replied.

"C'mon. She's my mom. I need to know."

"At least tell him something," Marty said in response to the anxious look on Mike's face.

The EMTs looked at each other. One nodded his permission. "She should be fine. Vitals are good, she's awake and alert, reflexes check out. She'll get a thorough examine at the hospital to confirm it, but after a few hours she should be good to go."

Mike visibly relaxed. "Thanks." He bent down, his mouth near his mother's ear. "Now that I know you're okay, I'll let that plastic puck remark pass," he whispered, "but remember, the paramedics on TV always say 'Try not to talk right now' to their patients."

"Michael," Stephanie said from behind a smile made up of clenched teeth, "you're being a brat."

"I don't want Mr. St. Claire to think I'm a nerdy loser. Work with me." Michael straightened and looked at Marty. "She really needs quiet." He turned back to his mother and patted her shoulder. "I really am worried about you moving around so much, so shhh. Lie still. Chill, okay?"

"Before I *chill*, no pun intended, I just would like to

know what happens next," Stephanie said. "I am not too happy about having to spend the next few hours in a truss."

Marty furrowed his brow with the change in the tone of her voice. "Don't worry, my insurance will take care of the hospital. And please tell me you're not thinking about suing me already," he suddenly added. "You just woke up."

"I wasn't unconscious," Stephanie corrected.

"Your eyes were closed when I first got to the ice."

"I was thinking."

"About suing me?"

"Not until now."

He saw her blue eyes flash. "You're angry."

"You think? I could be having a major medical infarction here and you're worried about a lawsuit!"

"What kind of medical infarction?"

"You know what, Hockey Boy," Stephanie said closing her eyes, "I think I'm just going to let you worry about that one."

Mike put his body between Marty and his mother. "Hockey Boy? Mom, that is so not cool."

Stephanie opened her eyes in response to her son's voice. "Nothing about this day has been cool. I have a headache, my stomach is tossing lunch around, and my jeans have frozen to my backside like a wet tongue on a metal pole."

Mike saw another smile slash across Marty's face. "Aw, jeez." He turned back toward the rink as the Zamboni rumbled by on the ice. "Maybe I can get that thing to run over me and put me out of my misery."

As Marty watched the ambulance leave the parking lot, he put the heels of his palms on his eyelids and pushed hard. What in the world was wrong with him? Having to agree with Mike, the unexpected appearance of his candid male instincts was definitely "so not cool." But he had to admit, Stephanie Thomas piqued his interest. She sure was cute when she was angry. Hell, he decided, she was beautiful. Normally he gravitated to blonds, but with those striking ice-blue eyes of hers and auburn hair sassy like her verve, he could make an exception in this case.

He felt a grin grow on his lips. Okay, he decided, he'd analyze the situation. He liked the dance of humor he saw in her eyes, and the way her smile kicked up a notch when she thought she was getting the better of him. Under other circumstances, meeting a woman like Stephanie had potential.

He called himself a few unflattering names for thinking about her in anything but concerned terms as he headed toward his car. However, as much as he hated to admit it, it may be a deep-seated sense of responsibility that had him heading to the hospital, but it would be an innate desire to learn more about Stephanie Thomas that would keep him there after he was sure she'd be all right.

The next time Marty saw Mike, it was in the waiting room at Somerset Hospital. Mike sat at the far wall, slouched in a blue plastic chair with shiny metal legs. Hat on backwards, arms across his chest, his body language shouted uncomfortable. He made a face in response to the daytime soap opera playing on the TV mounted high on the wall across from him.

"Hi," Marty said, easing himself into the empty chair next to Mike. "How's your mom?"

"Okay, I guess."

"Where is she?"

Mike nodded toward the hallway. "Down in one of those examining rooms."

"Why aren't you with her?"

"I tried a couple of dozen times, but some nurse who looks like Brunhilda kept chasing me back here to wait. I guess I'd probably be in the way." He glanced back at the ER desk. It was surrounded by people waiting to check in. "There is a lot of stuff going on, and I'm sure my mom won't leave without me."

"Guess we wait then." Marty glanced up at the TV. Two daytime soap stars were locked in a passionate kiss. From his angle, the actress looked a little like Mike's mother. As the TV angles moved around the couple, without his involvement or permission, his imagination suddenly took over the scene.

Mike's mother was in his arms, his hands moving through her silken hair. The strands slipped through his fingers like red satin ribbons as she tilted her head back. When she did not resist, he moved his hands down her back and pressed her closer, sculpting her body to his. He heard a small sigh escape her throat when he kissed the soft curve of her lower lip and felt her hands alternately open and close against his chest as he slowly kissed her more fully. He mapped the gentle arch of her spine with his fingertips and felt her surrender to—

"Hey! How can you watch that junk?"

Marty gave his head a quick shake when Mike's voice quickly dissolved the daydream. "Huh?"

"That junk. How can you watch it? I mean it isn't exactly Devils-Rangers."

"I wasn't watching it exactly. I was thinking about your mom." What on earth brought *that* on, anyway. An hour ago, he hadn't even known the woman existed, and now he was all over her like a warm, wool afghan on a cold day; even if only in his mind. He had to get himself, and his raging male instincts, together.

"Maybe we should see how she is," Marty suggested. He rose and started to walk toward the examining rooms. "You coming?" he asked when he noticed Mike wasn't following him.

Mike glanced up but didn't move. "Nah, I'll wait here. Watch out for Brunhilda. You can't miss her. She's lurking around here somewhere, and she's built like a Canadian defenseman."

Marty grimaced in response and walked down the hall.

Stephanie reclined on a gurney, the back of her right wrist resting across her forehead. With her eyes closed, she replayed the last few hours in her mind. Despite all her careful planning nothing had gone right. Mike would most likely not speak to her for a while, at least not until he needed something like lunch money or one of the latest T-shirts all the kids were wearing. He would definitely not agree to a family day any time soon, if ever again.

Looking back, maybe that "Hockey Boy" remark probably was not the smartest thing to say. She sighed. She'd have to try something else to get back in her son's good graces. But ever since he'd turned fifteen, and his teenage independence had kicked in, the job was getting harder and harder.

She heard the door open, but did not open her eyes. Her head still ached despite the pain medication she had been given, and the bright lights in the room only made her temples throb even harder. "Well, will I live?" she quipped to whomever entered the room.

"I sure hope so."

She recognized the voice. "Mr. St. Claire," she said lowering her arm. "What are you doing here?"

"Checking on you," he said casually, "and please, call me Marty."

"Marty then. They wouldn't let Mike in here. How did you manage?"

"If you act like you belong, I've found that people think you do."

"I tried that. I ended up on my butt on the ice."

Marty grinned. "A lot of people do that."

"I bet not too many of them end up in the emergency room."

His grin faded. "I wouldn't take that bet if I were you."

Just then the doctor came in and began examining Stephanie's ankle one more time. Marty stepped to the side and watched the doctor work. Stephanie took the opportunity to study him on the sly.

His jeans fit snugly across his hips and ended at new sneakers with blue check marks curling along the sides. He wore a well-worn leather jacket over a light blue shirt. He stood with feet widespread but firmly planted, both hands in the rear pockets of his jeans, the stance pulling his jacket open and hinting at a powerful, well-built frame. She had the fleeting thought that a man like him could probably walk into a room and wake a woman up from a coma, and wondered where it came from.

When he turned his head, his ruggedly attractive profile surprised her. A two-inch scar on the right side marred his forehead, but the warm tones of his skin seemed to mute the mark, making it look more like a shadow. The lights threw golden glints into hair that curled down to his collar, making her wonder what it would feel like spiraling across the back of her hand.

She had always felt men with longish hair looked a little feminine, but there was nothing effeminate about Martin St. Claire. Maybe it was the way he stood that made her sweep his length; shoulders back, chest out, athletically built, self-assured, perhaps a slight bit cocky. Or maybe she was giving him the once-over simply because it had been a long time since she felt this attracted to any man.

Marty caught her studying him. He winked and flashed a smile that transformed his face into an expression of complete charm. He did it so effortlessly that it made her wonder if it came from instinct or years of practice.

"Looks like you're free to go," Marty said, his eyes crinkling at the corners with his smile.

"Free?" She glanced past him and then realized the doctor had been speaking to her and she'd missed most of what he had said.

"You can leave."

"Oh. Yes. I know." But she hadn't. She was too busy ogling Martin St. Claire to pay attention to anyone else. The doctor had even wrapped her ankle in an Ace bandage and she hadn't felt a thing.

"I suggest you stay off that ankle for a day or two. You're going to need someone to drive you home," the ER doctor said.

"My car is at the rink," she said, scooting to the edge of the gurney. "I can call a cab."

"Is there someone you can call? Husband, boyfriend . . ." Marty hesitated.

A spark of something rose in his eyes making Stephanie feel as though he wanted her to fill in the blanks.

"No, no one, I mean, of course I have friends, but on a Friday afternoon I wouldn't want anyone to have to leave work or change any plans for me."

"Then I'll drive you and Mike home," Marty offered. "We can get the car later."

"Are you sure it won't be too much trouble?"

"It's the least I can do." He reached for the crutches a nurse brought in and held out his hand to help Stephanie into a waiting wheelchair.

As she looked at him a strange premonition mixed with the body vibrations already moving along the lines of her nerves. She could feel a trace of heat warm her cheeks. *Don't touch him,* she warned herself. *Remember what happened at the ice rink.* She shook off the feeling and blatantly ignored her own advice.

Taking his hand, she slid off the edge of the gurney and leaned against him. The sleeve of his jacket was cool, but the warmth of his skin seeped through it, making her aware of the solid body beneath. The sensation shot through her, stunning her with its intensity. She stumbled in reaction and he caught her. A refreshing scent of lemon soap mixed with an underlying musk filled her senses.

When he swept her effortlessly into the wheelchair, the scrape of his arms unwinding from around her body made her look up into his eyes. They were such an amazing color, one minute golden brown, another so dark that she could get lost in their depths if she wasn't careful. There could not possibly be a shade on any color chart that could describe them, she decided. As she continued to stare, she saw a sparkle of interest rise that took her breath away.

"I wish more women fell for me this easily," he said,

adjusting the footrests on the wheelchair. "Comfortable?"

She had no answer for him.

As he pushed her into the hall to meet Mike, a faraway voice issued a warning that slanted through her heart. *Watch out. The man's a flirt, a very practiced one at that, probably with a list of broken hearts as long as his hockey stick, with enough room left on it for my name.*

Chapter Two

"Oops." Marty jerked the wheelchair to a stop outside the double doors of the emergency room. With both hands, he caught Stephanie by the shoulders as she began to slide forward, but could do nothing to stop her purse from slipping onto the ground.

"Oops what?" Stephanie took her handbag from Mike and replaced it on her lap.

"I jumped in the Porsche to get here. I should have brought a bigger car."

"Don't worry," Stephanie replied. "I told you, I can take a cab to the ice rink and drive myself home." She got up but stumbled as she put weight on her ankle.

"I don't think so." Marty took her arm and eased her back to sitting with a gentle tug. "You'd have to crawl to the cab. Or I could carry you." He walked in front of her, leaned back, hands on hips. "Shouldn't be a problem. What are you, a hundred-twenty, hundred-thirty tops?"

"*Never*, under any circumstances, ask a woman her

19

age or her weight," Stephanie warned him. "If you do, there's a good chance you could end up on *your* back on a stretcher."

He laughed. "I like a woman who asserts herself."

"I have no problem in that area."

Mike had been listening to the exchange. He threw up his hands. "Aw jeez."

"Pardon my rude son," Stephanie said, giving Mike a warning glance. "We can manage to get home on our own."

"I'd feel better if you let me help you."

Mike suddenly stepped in between them. "Mom, I have to do that team project for history with Joey and Trey tonight. Joey lives just a couple of blocks from here. I can walk to his house while you two decide what you want to do here."

"Joey? I don't know him."

"He's a senior."

"That doesn't tell me very much."

"He's okay. He wears those pajama pants with the wild prints on them all the time."

"That's still not much of a resume unless you count a lack of fashion sense."

"He's harmless," Mike responded quickly.

Stephanie's shoulders tensed with the thought of another one of their test of wills coming on. "I'm not comfortable with not knowing him or where he lives."

"It's close. I promise." Mike glanced at Marty before looking back at his mom. "I *am* old enough to walk the streets in broad daylight."

"I never said you weren't."

"Then it's settled." Mike slapped his hands together and began walking away. "I won't be late."

"Michael, call me when you get there," Stephanie called after him in a desperate attempt to exert some authority.

Mike acknowledged her with a wave of his hand.

"Wait! I need the address," she shouted, watching him disappear around the corner of the building. As she stood to go after him, her leg tangled with the wheelchair's footrest and, stumbling, she grabbed onto the nearest thing for stability. It was Marty.

As soon as she touched him, her female reaction switches rotated to the 'on' position again. When he slipped his free arm around her waist to steady her, heat exploded inside her chest. When he kicked the wheelchair aside so she wouldn't crash into it, her heart beat faster. When he nestled her against his hip for support, she almost forgot to breathe.

She looked at him. His smile had enough mischief in it to make her feel as though he had set the whole thing up.

"You tend to fall a lot," he said through his smile.

"Seems that way lately."

"Mike leaving solves our seating problem," Marty said as he eased her back into the wheelchair. "Wait here. I'll get the car."

While Stephanie watched Marty walk away, she realized she was fast developing a curious fascination with him. Maybe it was because he was the first man in a long time that seemed to have piqued her interest. Maybe that scar of his made him look like a bad boy, an interesting and dangerous bad boy. And yes, maybe the way he made her feel when he touched her had muddled her mind. She could feel the warmth rise on her cheeks as for a moment, one silly moment, she thought she might be looking at the man of her dreams.

And because it was such a ridiculous notion, she folded her arms over her chest, looked down at the sidewalk and laughed out loud.

"Would you like to come in?" Stephanie leaned her hip against the wrought iron railing on her porch, the tip of her right foot barely touching the cement porch. She turned the key and opened the front door to her small Cape Cod-style home. "I'm not sure what condition the place is in. Mike and I barely have time to keep ourselves in clean towels with the schedule we have these days." She pushed the door open, careful to transfer most of the weight to her left leg.

"For a minute. To make sure you're settled," Marty replied, holding the door open for her with a stiff-arm move and watching as she ducked under his forearm to get inside. "I still have to get to the rink before everyone goes home. I need to get someone to follow me while I drive your car back here."

Stephanie flicked on the light switch just inside the door. She looked around. "Just as I feared. It's pretty messy in here. Find yourself a chair that doesn't have something on it and I'll be right out." She slowly walked to the back of the house trying her best to disguise the limp and disappeared with a right turn in the rear hallway as Marty stepped inside.

"Looks homey," he called after her. "It's very nice."

Stephanie came back into view and hung her coat in a small closet in the center of the back wall before continuing down the hallway to the left as she spoke. "I'd give you a tour, but there isn't much to see. You're in the living room. Kitchen's behind me, half-bathroom's next to it." She reappeared near the closet. She pointed to the left. "That way used to be two small rooms, but I had a contractor take out the wall and make it into one large enough to hold all of Mike's sports gear and the computer. Upstairs are two bedrooms and a full bath."

Marty nodded. "Shouldn't you be sitting down with that ankle up on a bench or something?"

"Probably." She pointed to the couch. "If you toss that stuff on the floor, it looks like there'll be enough room for us both."

Marty heard the refrigerator door open and close as he set some magazines on the hassock before easing himself down onto the blue plaid sofa. "I have experience with bruised limbs. Your ankle's going to swell if you don't get off it soon and ice it down like the doctor told you to do."

"I was thinking the same thing." Stephanie walked into the living room, a bag of frozen peas in her hand. "I'm out of ice," she said in reply to the puzzled look on Marty's face. She sat down next to him. "Could you slide over the chair? The one with the granny-squared afghan on it."

Marty complied.

Stephanie propped her leg up on the chair cushion and draped the bag of peas across her ankle.

"I'm sure when Emeril thinks of peas, he doesn't think of them as medicinal," Marty quipped.

"You look like you're afraid I may cook them up and try to feed them to you."

"After a day like today, nothing would surprise me!"

They both laughed, stopped, and laughed again.

"I assure you, that won't happen," she said. "I think these have been in the freezer a few years and are not much use for anything else. I have to remember to pick up that ice thing with the blue stuff inside to put in the freezer for emergencies. With all the bangs and dings Mike gets during a hockey game, we pretty much are used to using frozen food on swelling."

"So after the peas thaw out, you'll put the bag back on ice?"

She wiggled her toes. "Yeah, works for me."

"You're something, Stephanie Martin. Some people would be on the phone to their lawyer starting a lawsuit against the rink, but instead, you're sitting in your living room with legumes on your leg."

"You get sued a lot?"

"I have a few times since I opened the rink, but mostly the insurance company settles any claims." He blew out a long breath of air. "Until last week."

"What happened last week?"

"Got canceled."

"Oh," Stephanie's mouth stayed pursed as she contemplated what he said. "Canceled, huh?"

He waved his hands in a defensive gesture. "No, it's okay. I bought re-insurance a few days ago so you're covered under that." He tossed his head. "It's written for high risk businesses." He looked at her ankle. "I don't think frozen food is covered though." His laugh seemed to begin somewhere deep inside his chest before it reached his lips.

His smile unearthed a wellspring of reactions in her. Laughter again bubbled up in her throat, along with a churning that crackled inside her stomach. She almost forgot the embarrassing way she had met him and became glad that she had.

She settled back into the cushions. "Well, I'm not going to sue you, and I can buy my own peas."

"Even though people have to sign a waiver, I've had six cases filed against me this year alone."

She grimaced. "Bummer."

He nodded. "They were all dismissed, but now the insurance costs have gone through the roof with the rink now being covered by New Jersey-Re." He shrugged. "But I knew the financial risks associated with opening an ice rink."

"Why open one here in central Jersey instead of somewhere closer to the New York market?"

"Actually, the public relations consultant I had during my NHL career suggested that I build one closer to the Meadowlands."

"Why didn't you?"

"I thought a rural setting would give more people an opportunity to enjoy the ice the way I do. Whether it was in competition sports like hockey or figure skating, or just circling with friends on the ice during a public skating session, I wanted as many people as possible to be able to take advantage of finding out how much fun they can have."

Stephanie looked at her ankle. "Yeah, fun."

"I don't mean on the ice the way you were," Marty said in reaction to her body language. "I meant more like actually on the skate blades."

Laughter came easily when he described the peewee hockey teams with their four and five-year-old players, and the way the kids spent more time down on the ice than up on their skates. As he continued to tell stories about the ice rink, a fair amount of cavalier flirtation became inevitable.

"I would have thought we would have met at one of your son's hockey games," he said. "I frequently check in on the high school teams to make sure no one is getting too rough with the checks."

"I don't get to many games. My job keeps me pretty busy." Her gaze wandered from his eyes to his lips for a brief moment before she forced herself to look away. "But I did promise him I'd try to go more."

"Hockey can be an expensive sport. What do you do to help pay for his ice time and equipment and the like?"

"I work for a local PR firm doing advertising and marketing for local merchants."

"Tough business. Do you like it?"

"It pays the bills and leaves me enough for this palatial mansion with all these original oil paintings." She swept her hand in the air and pointed to the one on the way across from them. "Like that one. I think it's called *Dogs at a Poker Game*. It's Mike's." She shifted her gaze to her hands folded in her lap. "But I guess you are used to originals and first editions."

"Not necessarily. I actually have velvet Elvis in my office at the house. A fan sent it to me. She told me it was her good luck charm and if I hung it up, we were guaranteed to win. I hung it and won my third Stanley Cup with the New Jersey Devils that year."

"That would be something to see among your trophies and plaques."

"It's there. You'll have to come by sometime and check it out."

"Curiosity alone may force me to take you up on that." She stopped abruptly as a warning voice inside her head took over. *Stephanie Martin, stop it. You're openly flirting with the man.*

"Good, we'll have to arrange a private viewing," Marty replied. He shifted and threw an arm across the back of the couch.

The commonplace action captivated Stephanie, her reaction to such a simple movement surprising her. She countered by scooting back toward the armrest, knocking the makeshift ice bag from her ankle as she did.

"I'll get it." Marty dropped to one knee. He picked up the clammy bag and put it back on her ankle. It promptly slid back onto the floor. After another try with the same results, he attempted to even out the saggy weight by jostling the bag a few times before placing it vertically on her leg.

Stephanie looked at him and shook her head. "It's not my shin that hurts."

"This is harder than trying to win a faceoff."

They reached for the bag at the same time but grabbed each other's hand instead. The peas slid back onto the floor with a dull clunk. Neither Stephanie nor Marty appeared to notice.

Stephanie's heart fluttered as they began to slide their hands apart and then stopped. Their fingers entwined again, the pressure of Marty's touch tentative, gentle, as though he was letting her get used to the presence of his hand on hers rather than just grabbing on. She could feel the heat from his hand. His fingers were long, solid, with the nicks and mars that came from playing hockey. The aroma of his lemon-scented cologne surrounded her along with a sense that they were hovering on the brink of something that was not wise to begin.

Marty stood, still holding her hand in his. He put his free hand on the back of the sofa next to her head. Releasing her hand, he brushed a stray lock of auburn hair from her eyes.

"Mike should be calling any minute. I should . . ." She tipped her head and leaned against the back of the loveseat as his fingertips caressed her hairline.

"I know," he agreed tenderly as he began to lower his mouth to hers.

She could feel vibrations flutter across the back of her neck through the coarse fabric of the sofa as though Marty was using it as a brace to hold back. A part of her started to hold back too, not wanting him to think that she was too eager. *Don't think so much,* an impulsive voice inside her head said, *just do it.* Listening to the voice, she put her hands on either side of his forearms, closed off her brain to all logical communication and pulled him closer.

His lips touched hers in a warm, slow connection. As the intensity grew, her pulse began to hammer, and her nerves sparked up and down her spine. She took pleasure in the way his lips felt on hers and became too mindless to react the way she should have to a man she just met and hardly knew. She enjoyed kissing him like this, and kiss him she did until all too soon it was over.

When they parted he turned and lowered himself next to her onto the sofa. "So . . ." he said, pulling in a jerky breath.

"So," she repeated.

The air in the room seemed supercharged with temptation.

"As your son so aptly put it at the rink, that was so not cool, right?"

She pressed her lips together and took pleasure in the warmth she still felt. "I have to admit, my ankle feels much better now." Hoping her voice sounded pragmatic, she reached for the nearly forgotten bag of peas and tossed it onto a nearby chair. But she suspected she didn't fool him. They had both reacted the same way to the kiss. She felt it.

"That's a good thing, right?"

Stephanie nodded. "Took my mind off the pain for a while."

She saw his eyes reheat. "I had this feeling almost from the moment I saw you that you would be trouble for me," he said.

"You're blaming me for this?"

"Uh-huh." His smile came up again.

"You might be used to women falling all over you, but I only tripped, remember."

"As I said, you seem to fall a lot."

"Surely you don't think I planned this?"

"I'd be flattered if you did."

"I suppose some women would have gone to such lengths to get your attention, but none of this would have ever happened if I didn't try to skate with Mike today."

"I'm glad Mike plays hockey then. Otherwise we may have never met."

She tossed her head, fully intending to snap out a sassy comeback, but his smile had kicked like a solar flare, interfering with the signals in her response center. She wasn't falling for his lines, she told herself. Maybe his kiss had tripped up her sanity and maybe she thought he was an incredibly handsome man, but she was far too practical to think anything could happen between them. *Enough with these ridiculous thoughts,* she commanded her mind. She needed to focus on something else.

"And speaking of Mike," she said as a defense against her own senses, "he should be calling any second."

"Nice segue."

She smiled. He was going to gallantly let her change the tone of their conversation. "As long as I'm on the subject of my son, let me apologize for his rudeness this

afternoon. He's," she searched for the right word,
". . . hormonal right now. I can't seem to do anything
right in his eyes these days."

Marty settled back on the sofa. "It must be tough
having to work and deal with a teenager."

"It's an adventure."

"Do you have anyone to help you?"

"Like who?"

"A serious boyfriend maybe?"

Stephanie furrowed her brows. "That seems like a
question you should have asked before you kissed me."

"Probably, but I'm making this up as I go along, so
I'm not clear on the correct order of things."

"I find that hard to believe coming from someone like
you."

"Being . . . ," he searched for the word, ". . . popular,"
he laughed, "isn't all it's cracked up to be."

"Hmm," she said with a touch of disbelief in her tone.
"Let me give you a quick lesson then. Meet first. Small
talk, about her, about you. Flirt. Date. Then the other
stuff comes in. Maybe."

"Sounds like you've done this before."

"Not a lot." She sighed her answer. "But I am reading
up on the subject."

"Maybe we can learn a few things together."

"I see you're already into the flirting part, and I'd love
to participate, but I am beginning to worry about Mike.
He should have called or been home by now. I should
call around to some of his friends and check on him."

"Should I leave?"

She shook her head. "I'll only be a second."

She began to walk toward the kitchen to use the phone
hanging on the wall next to the refrigerator when the

front door banged open. A blur in a hockey jersey flew up the flight of steps. In another second, a door slammed upstairs.

Stephanie had barely taken two wobbly strides toward the staircase when the front of the room exploded with light. Brilliant bursts of red, white, and blue pulsated through the sheer curtains that hung on the bay window, capturing everything in an eerie glow.

Stephanie stood immobile, open-mouthed, as pounding on the front door was accompanied by a deep, distinctly male voice shouting, "It's the police. Open up."

Chapter Three

Stephanie yanked open the front door of her home. "What did you say?" She blinked hard a few times and then looked back and forth between the officer standing on her porch and Marty standing beside her. Marty grimaced. The officer remained stoic.

"Ma'am, if you're Stephanie Thomas, the owner of that car in the driveway," the policeman replied, tossing his head toward the Mustang, "I need to speak with you and the person who ran into this house a second ago."

"Last time I saw my car it was parked at the ice rink," she said, glancing over the officer's shoulder at the irrefutable evidence. She sighed, letting her shoulders drop. "I guess not anymore."

"Yes, ma'am. The car was moving erratically, the driver doing twenty-five in a fifty zone and pumping on the brakes. I ran the plates and when I turned on the lights to pull the car over, the driver suddenly sped up and turned the car in here." He looked at her wrapped ankle. "I'm guessing you weren't driving."

Stephanie felt herself get lightheaded. She raised both hands in a defensive move, and beckoned for Marty and the officer to follow her. "You're going to have to come in because I have to sit down."

They walked into the kitchen. She almost fell into the chair when she tried to sit. She slid her elbows onto the table and made small circles in the air with one hand.

Marty and the policeman looked at each other with furrowed brows.

"Water," she whispered.

In one long stride from the table, Marty got to the kitchen cabinets and began ripping open the doors. On the third try he found a glass and filled it for her. Stephanie motioned for everyone to sit while she finished the water in two large gulps. Marty complied, but the policeman declined with a polite shake of his head.

She set the glass down with a thump. "Tell me again what my car did?"

"I was in the patrol car going east on Green Street when a car, the one in your driveway, passed me going west. I noticed it was traveling way under the speed limit and, when I looked in my rearview mirror, I saw the brake lights going off and on. I thought maybe the driver was in trouble, so I did a K-turn and caught up to the vehicle just as it pulled in to your driveway. I saw the person in the driver's seat run in here."

Stephanie's eyes widened. "Maybe the car was stolen and the prep . . ."

"Perp?" Marty asked skeptically.

"Yes. *The perp*, could have used the registration to find the house and is upstairs hiding right this minute."

"Stef, I don't think a car thief would lead an officer in pursuit to the owner's house and then run upstairs and hide under the bed," Marty offered.

Calmly, the patrolman pulled out his pad. "Who else could have been driving your car?" The officer glanced around the room, a school varsity jacket hung on a hook near the back door, and some schoolbooks lay on the counter. "A son perhaps?"

Stephanie stood again and grabbed at a dishtowel from the towel rack. She swiped at the counter as she spoke. "Yes. But Michael's at a friend's house right now." She whisked dirty glasses from the sink into the dishwasher.

"Maybe I should talk to your son."

Stephanie stopped wiping the counters and turned slowly.

"If he's home, ma'am," the officer quickly added after seeing the troubled look on her face.

She sighed heavily. "I suspect he is. I'll get him."

As she walked toward the center hall staircase, she vacillated between angry and worried. She thought she'd been doing a good job of juggling work and her family life. She thought she had kept a close enough eye on Mike, and knew him well enough to be certain that he had nice friends and would use commonsense when she wasn't around. However, apparently she and Michael had different definitions of safety and security these days. The danger of the times and her worry about them crept up from the back of her mind. What had she missed?

She reached the top of the stairs. The door to Mike's room was ajar. She knocked twice on the door.

"Come in, Mom."

She swept the door open, leaned against the frame and crossed her arms over her chest. "Expecting me?"

Mike nodded. He sat on his bed, head down, forearms resting on his thighs, fingers interlaced.

"Want to tell me about it?"

He looked up. His gaze locked with hers and he swallowed. "Am I under arrest?"

Stephanie shrugged. "I don't know. Maybe." She saw him pale.

"I've really screwed up, haven't I?"

"Looks that way. What happened?"

He sat up and then dropped backward onto the bed, throwing an arm over his eyes as he spoke. "Man, I don't know. One minute we were all at Joey's doing history, the next minute, I'm a convicted felon."

"I think you left out a few important steps between freedom and your impending trek to the county jail." Stephanie walked over to the bed and sat down. With the pressure, Mike hoisted himself up onto his elbows and looked at her. "Come on, out with it," she urged. "I promise I won't testify against you."

Mike hesitated, but then slowly began. "Joey has his permit, you know. I told him what happened and that your car was still at the rink. He asked if I had a set of keys and I said no but—"

"But you told him you knew where I hid the spare."

Michael nodded and then stared up at the poster of the Dave Matthews Band that he had taped onto the ceiling above his bed. "Joey said he could drive it home for you and Trey thought it was a good idea."

Stephanie scooted back and rested her knee on the edge of the bed. "But what did you think?"

Michael fell back and pulled part of a bunched up blue comforter over his eyes. "Apparently I didn't."

"Go on."

Mike uncovered his face. "Well, Trey, he's a senior, too, and, you know, has a car. He drove us to the rink and then left. I showed Joey where the key was and we got in. Everything was fine until Joey's mom called him on his cell and started yelling at him for something. He said he had to go home right then."

"So he drove the car to his house?"

"Are you kidding? His mom would have killed him if she knew he was driving on his permit without a licensed driver in the car."

"Really?" Stephanie made sure her voiced was laced with just the right amount of sarcasm. "Then what happened?"

"Well Joey pulled over and called Trey on his cell. Trey came and they left."

"Where were you and the car then?"

"On Amsterdam."

"Five blocks. Why didn't you just walk home and leave the car there?"

"I don't know. I guess because it was just five blocks."

"I can't let this go, Mike."

He nodded.

"You were totally irresponsible."

"I know."

"Someone could have gotten hurt."

Mike pressed his lips together and looked at her. "I know that too."

"Mike, it's just us. You and me. We've always been a team, and now that you're getting older, I should be able to trust you and be comfortable knowing you're making the right decisions. But this little joy ride of yours tells me that you have a way to go and I have a lot more work to do to help you with it."

"Mom, I'm sorry."

"Sorry isn't enough. You know that there have to be consequences. And I don't mean just those the police officer downstairs are going to lay out to you."

"I know, I screwed up."

"Royally."

"You hate me, right?"

Stephanie moved closer to him and he sat up. "Of course not. I love you." She put an arm around his shoulders and felt him relax. "But don't mistake my composure right now with acceptance. I'm very upset but I can assure you this, you are not going to forget what you did tonight for a very long time."

Michael glanced at the doorway over her shoulder. "Mom, what's going to happen to me?"

"I honestly don't know." Stephanie stood. "What I do know is that there is an angry police officer in my kitchen and I think you need to talk to him."

"Are you mad?"

"Furious."

"I thought as much."

"But not mad enough to let you get taken out of here in handcuffs with a raincoat over your head." She saw Michael's eyes widen to the size of dessert plates.

"Mom, I—"

She silenced him with a swipe of one hand. "The officer is not leaving until you talk to him." She put an arm around her son's shoulders and could feel him shaking. "Listen, I don't know what to do about this right now. But I do know that I have your back. We'll figure something out, okay?"

Mike looked up at her. She could see a small sense of relief darting around in his eyes. "I'm sorry, Mom."

Stephanie kissed the top of his head. "Honey, you haven't even begun to be sorry about this one."

"What do you think is happening in there?" Stephanie began to get up from the sofa, but Marty stopped her with a hand to her shoulder.

"I think Officer Livak is giving Mike a much needed lecture on what could have happened to him and to others," he replied.

"I wish I knew what was going to happen after that."

Marty settled back on the couch. "While you were upstairs getting Mike, Officer Livak and I had a little chat about the situation. I think what's going to happen is that Mike will get what the officer called a 'station-house adjustment.' "

Stephanie furrowed her brows. "What's that?"

"Mike will have to talk to the juvenile officer about what he did."

"That's all?"

"I think so. I told Officer Livak that I knew Mike from hockey and that he's a good kid who probably just had a small lapse of good judgment considering everything that happened today."

"Officer Livak agreed?"

"It's not like the officer has never been fifteen once. And he's never seen Mike before, so he probably figured it was the first time anything like this has ever happened. Mike's a good kid and deserves a break."

"But you only know Mike from hockey, how do you know he's a good kid?"

"I think I know enough to make a pretty decent judgment call."

Stephanie leaned her elbow on the armrest and shifted backward. "Just what do you think you know anyway?"

Marty mimicked her move. "Everything about you reeks of the conventional. You're strong, honest, caring. There was no bloodletting when you went upstairs to get Mike, so it seems you're willing to listen. And you're creative."

Stephanie relaxed her body language. "You can tell all that by looking at me?"

"All except for the creative part. I got that from the bag of peas." She laughed and he liked the way it sounded. "Seriously," he continued, "I got all that by spending the better part of the day with you." He threw his arm across the back of the sofa. "As a pro hockey player, maybe any pro player, you have to learn to read people fast. Like during the faceoff of a game. You have maybe a few seconds to look across at the opposing player and sense if he's confident, or anxious, or distracted by something that happened that day. Guess right and you have the edge. Guess wrong and he does. After a while you learn to look at a person and just know."

Stephanie shot him a wry look. "I'm supposed to believe that malarkey?"

She saw a dance of humor in his eyes. "Officer Livak did."

About that time, the officer came into the room. Stephanie bolted to standing. Marty rose much slower.

"I think we're done for tonight," he said.

Stephanie looked past him. Mike sat at the kitchen table, eyes cast down, hands folded on the tabletop. "What happens next?"

"You'll have to bring your son down to the station to talk to the juvenile officer. He'll take it from there."

"Do I make an appointment or something?" Stephanie asked, walking the officer to the door.

"You should call to get his schedule."

Nervously, she slid her hands into her back pockets. She wasn't sure whether to shake his hand or not. "Thanks. Thanks for everything," she said.

Officer Livak nodded. "I'm just glad no one got hurt."

"Me too."

Marty reached around her and extended his hand. "We'll make sure Mike gets to the station."

"Let me know if I can do anything for you," Officer Livak acknowledged with a returning firm handshake. He shifted his gaze to Stephanie. "Your son stepped right up and accepted the responsibility for what he did. Kids his age usually don't do that."

"I appreciate your telling me that." Stephanie looked down at the hardwood floor and then quickly back up at the officer. "I guess I'll have to keep a closer eye on him."

Officer Livak nodded. "Yes, ma'am. Good night then."

After the door closed Stephanie leaned her forehead against it and let out a long sigh. "You can't make this stuff up," she quipped. She turned and rested on the door, hands behind her back. "Now comes the hard part."

"Of being a parent?" Marty moved to her until they were toe to toe.

"Of being anything when there's a teenager in the house."

"Oh, I think you'll survive."

"I'm glad you were here, Marty. I can't put it into words, but it helped somehow."

"Good."

His palm touched her cheek and she lifted her face. Something was there; an expression that made her heart leap. The connection between them strengthened as his fingers began to caress her jaw. She did not move away, but met his gaze with the wariness of a first date. He leaned forward to kiss her and then stopped, seemingly to give her a chance to decline. When she still didn't move away, he moved forward again.

His lips touched hers and she realized almost immediately that this wasn't like any other kiss. Whisper soft, it felt right, like they belonged together. She thought there had to be a catch and kept waiting for the crazy connection between them to dissolve. Only it didn't. His mouth trailed a path of kisses from her lips to her throat and she heard herself sigh.

The heels of his hands slid to her side, his touch light. His fingertips traced her ribs and anticipation burned through her. Then slower than honey pouring from a jar, his mouth lifted from her skin. His cheek nuzzled hers and she opened her eyes. They stared at each other like a couple of teenagers waiting for their parents to come in.

"Well, that was totally inappropriate at a time like this," he said moving back a step. "I seem to be giving a new meaning to 'totally not cool.' I didn't plan for that to happen again. Somehow I get a bit out of control when I'm around you."

"I didn't think that you had."

"I originally intended to make sure you were settled at home and that you were comfortable."

Stephanie grinned. "I'm very comfortable."

"Me too." He looked into her eyes and waited for the chemistry between them to either explode or fizzle. It did neither, just bubbled at a level that made him edgy and aware.

Stephanie dropped her gaze. "I really should talk to Mike."

He nodded. "And I should be going." He ambled to the door. "If you need anything, call. Okay?"

"Uh-huh."

She watched him walk to his car through the small window in the center of the door. She had to admit, she felt a little out of control herself when she was around him. Was she being a terrible mother for enjoying the way she felt around Marty? Her rusty hormones had kicked up into a gear they hadn't seen for quite some time and she liked the way it felt. But as much as it tempted her, she was not going to leap and follow the impulse that jolted every one of her senses. She had no time to be impressed with Marty's smile or his glib tongue right now.

She had a son to interrogate.

Chapter Four

The Coreman Group's receptionist quit on Friday, which was just as well because Stephanie was sure that the owner was going to fire the young woman anyway. But now she had double duty until a new one was hired.

Stephanie sat at the chipped mahogany desk, plopped an elbow on the At-A-Glance calendar on the desktop and looked around the room. Devoid of any amenities, it was simple yet functional. Much like her life. Her salary at the PR firm paid the bills, but left little for luxuries. But that was okay with her.

She didn't need plush carpets or highly polished matching furniture with soft leather chairs. The well-used desk and equally well-used bookcase in her office made her feel as comfortable as she felt in her small saltbox house and her blue economy car. She didn't need the flash and pomp of a larger firm. Here she felt useful and productive.

Other aspects of the job suited her too. She liked looking out the window and seeing the local traffic go by.

She liked being able to walk to the corner deli and pick up lunch in five minutes for less than five dollars. In many ways she liked the feeling of being settled.

She stood and smoothed the skirt of her navy-blue off-the-rack suit, adjusted the jacket and shifted from receptionist to ad executive. If potential clients came in, she'd hear them walking up the wooden stairs. The fourth step creaked like the Tin Man in the Wizard of Oz.

A few strides down the narrow hallway and she was in her own office. Small, almost like an afterthought, it seemed squeezed into the back of the old building right next to the bathroom with bad plumbing. But that was okay with her too.

She took the spindly ivy plant from her desk and set it on the windowsill, hoping the morning sun might revive it. Maybe today she could restart some of her old accounts as well.

She had hit a slow spot. The Wednesday before she took a header on the ice, she'd cleaned off her desk and finished inputting the last of her sales into the computer she shared with Tina, the owner's secretary. The small newspaper ads didn't take much effort or ability to sell and, so far, nothing else had come in. Thank heavens she had a base pay, so at least that meant a steady paycheck. But it also meant that she'd probably spend most of the coming week on the phone checking in with clients she hadn't heard from in a while.

Mentally she made a list of expenses she could put off until someone bought a full-page ad she could design and sell to one of the local magazines. Her dishwasher was on the fritz, but with some elbow power and a few new dishtowels, repairs could wait. The car had been making a few noises lately, but until a light popped on or a gauge went out of control, she'd nurse that along. And Mike needed some new hockey sticks . . .

Mike. She hit her forehead with the heel of her hand. She'd meant to ask Mr. Coreman for the afternoon off to take Mike to see the juvenile officer. When she got in Mr. Coreman seemed a bit grumpy, so she had decided to wait until after he had his morning coffee. Angling her watch to her eyes, she realized that had been two hours ago. Maybe if she begged.

She was still chastising herself for not being more prepared when Tina walked in flipping through the dog-eared pages of the yellow legal pad she was carrying.

Tina grinned. "Heard about your adventures on skates." She leaned against the doorjamb and tucked the pad under her arm, the movement momentarily wrinkling her white silk blouse until she noticed and moved the pad back into her hand. "I also heard Martin St. Claire spent an hour or so with you at the hospital. I'd trade a bruised butt for some one-on-one time with him."

Stephanie held up a finger as the phone began to ring. "The Coreman Group, Stephanie Thomas speaking." She paused. "Yes, we'd love to talk to you about promoting your business." She glanced at the desk calendar. The only thing she had scheduled for the week was a date with her hairdresser, but she paused for effect. "Hmm, I can fit you in tomorrow, say around two. Great. See you then."

Tina tossed her head. "New client?"

"Hope so."

"Why not get him in here this afternoon?"

Stephanie grimaced. "I can't be here this afternoon, and I don't want Bill to snag the account. I need the business."

"Enough shop talk. Back to St. Claire. What's that hunky model of male perfection like?"

"Male perfection?"

"Wait here." Tina spun on her heels, her long black hair moving like a veil across her back. She came back in three seconds waving a magazine. "Look at this." She dropped the periodical on Stephanie's desk. "In color so vivid, I could swear he's breathing."

"He's in *GQ*?" Stephanie asked. The question came out in a whisper.

"Not just in *GQ, on* the cover." Tina drummed a manicured finger on the shiny paper, careful not to get a mark near Marty's picture. "Look at that face. Rugged, yet dreamy. And those eyes." She picked up the magazine and turned it first one way and then the other. "This way they look brown, this way kind of greenish."

Stephanie sighed. "I know."

Tina didn't appear to hear her. "If you can tear yourself away from the dimple on his right cheek, turn to page forty-two. There's a whole spread on him."

Slowly Stephanie took the magazine from Tina's hands and opened it. She leafed through the pages until she got to the cover story, CANADIAN-BORN MARTY ST. CLAIRE, PRINCE CHARMING OF THE NHL.

The piece on him took up six pages, replete with pictures of Marty that showed perfection. There were shots of Marty in his living room, photos of him in the kitchen serving a cup of coffee to a woman. But the one that really caught her eyes was the picture of Marty in a tuxedo with another beautiful woman on his arm. She skimmed the article and caught words like, supermodels, Lear Jet, and friendships with people like Steven Spielberg and Prince Sameh of Egypt.

"That's not all," Tina said. "In this month's issue of *People* magazine, he's been voted one of the Fifty Most Beautiful People of the Year."

Stephanie closed the magazine and slowly lifted her head, tearing her gaze away from the sparkle in Marty's eyes. Tina reached over and put her forefinger under Stephanie's chin, helping her to close her mouth.

She gave her head a little shake and pulled herself together. "I had no idea about any of this. He seemed so normal."

"Define normal," Tina challenged.

"Normal, like just another guy."

"You're telling me that nothing jumped out at you to give you a clue that he wasn't the guy next door?"

"Okay, he drove a Porsche, but he was wearing faded jeans, a T-shirt, Nikes, and a leather jacket. He could have been the high school gym teacher for all I knew. He seemed to be your everyday average nice guy."

"Hello, there are pictures of him on Mike's wall," Tina said. "You didn't notice?"

"I noticed, but I didn't think about all the notoriety at the time."

"Maybe you can get him to let us take a tour of his estate. I've always wanted to see the inside of one of those huge houses in the Hills."

"He has an estate?"

"Read the article. He has a lot of stuff, including apparently, Kaylee McReynolds."

"The Victoria's Secret Model?"

"I think that was her with him on page forty-five."

Stephanie crossed her wrists on top of the desk and dropped her head onto them. "What a jerk I am."

Tina slipped into the chair against the wall. "What did you do? Spill it."

Stephanie looked up. "What makes you think I did anything?"

"The expression on your face."

"You don't miss much, do you?"

"I'm an executive assistant. I'm paid to observe and react."

Stephanie straightened and then slouched down in her chair. "I let him drive me home from the hospital."

"No."

"Yes." She covered her eyes with her hands. "Then I let him into my house. Actually gave him a tour. He seemed interested, but I guess he was probably only being polite. From looking at the magazine pictures, it appears my entire house can fit into his living room." She dropped her hands into her lap. "I can only imagine what he thought."

"Did he see the dog picture?"

She nodded. "He said he had a velvet Elvis," she said in defense.

Tina patted Stephanie on the top of her head. "Don't worry, your house is charming."

"Charming is what you say when you can't think of a word that won't hurt someone's feelings. My house is pitiful compared to his . . . ," she said as she grabbed the magazine and found the page she wanted, ". . . his eighteen-room home in the Hills. Eighteen rooms. Can you imagine? Why does a single man need all that space? I can barely keep six plus a bathroom the size of a small closet clean."

"He probably needs it so all the supermodels he's dating don't run into each other on weekends."

"Yeah," she said as she turned the page of the magazine and angled it to Tina, "at the backyard barbeque near the waterfall." She sighed. "But that's not the worst of it."

Tina stared at her for a long moment. "What happened?"

"I let him kiss me," Stephanie replied in the smallest voice she could manage.

"You let him trick you?"

Stephanie blew out a long breath of air. "I let him kiss me," she said louder.

Tina slammed her hand down on the desk so hard the mug Stephanie used as a penholder fell over. "Shut up! You did not!"

"I did," Stephanie admitted, stopping a few pens from rolling onto the floor and then scooping them back into the cup.

Tina propped on elbow on the desk and rested her chin in her hand. "Tell me everything," she said just as the squeak of the fourth step on the staircase indicated a caller.

Stephanie felt herself relax. "Some other time. I have to turn into the receptionist at the moment."

Chapter Five

Later that day, Marty tried to convince himself that the reason he pulled into Stephanie's driveway instead of going straight home from the ice rink was simply to make sure she was all right. She had to be dealing with a lot, most of it indirectly his doing. For that reason, he surmised, it was perfectly reasonable for him to stop by and see how she was making out.

Maybe.

Or it could have been the memory of those blue eyes of hers that brought him here. Or maybe her spirit and sense of humor. Better yet, it could be the way she made him feel; like he wanted to protect her, be there for her, especially since she looked so vulnerable on the stretcher and in the hospital bed.

But none of that had anything to do with it, he managed to rationalize. Considering his ice had started the chain reaction of events that caused her recent problems, he had to make sure nothing else bad happened.

He saw the curtains on the living room window flutter

as though someone had been peeking out, and decided it didn't matter why he came. He couldn't very well back out of the driveway, turn tail and run now anyway.

As he pushed open the car door and got out, Stephanie opened her front door and let out a tall, dark-haired man. With only a glance in Marty's direction, the man said something to Stephanie before she laughed and touched his arm. He then walked to a silver BMW parked near the curb that Marty had failed to notice. As Stephanie's visitor got into his car, she acknowledged Marty and began to walk toward him.

A black cat darted out from under the BMW as it started up, and ran across the street. Must be an omen, Marty concluded as he gave himself a mental whack on his head. He shouldn't be here. No thirty-eight-year-old man with half a brain should assume a woman like Stephanie would be alone. It was only logical that she had someone to turn to for comfort and encouragement. Someone like Stephanie would definitely not be lacking male company. He had probably interrupted a tender moment, and he felt quite awkward about it.

"This is a surprise, Marty," Stephanie said as she met him halfway.

Her voice almost knocked his knees out from under him like a defenseman's stick caught in his skates. He glanced at the disappearing tails lights of the BMW. "I didn't mean to chase anyone off. If this is a bad time, I can come back."

"No, it's fine," Stephanie assured.

"Boyfriend?"

"Colleague from the office dropping off some paper-work I need to go over tonight."

Marty felt the knot inside his stomach relax and hoped

the relief didn't show on his face. "How did things go at juvie?"

She laughed. "Sounds as though you know something about these things."

"Oh, I've broken a few windows in my day," Marty replied. "And threw one or two wild parties when the parents weren't home."

"Ah, disturbing the peace." She crossed her arms over her chest and nodded knowingly.

Her smile had a lot of mischief in it. Enough to distract him and make him feel as though he'd been hit with a slap shot. Disturbing the peace was about right. But only it was his peace, and she was the one shattering it.

"You could say that," he acknowledged.

"It wasn't all that bad. Mike got his 'station house adjustment' and I got a stiff lecture about the importance of structure in the teenage years."

"No jail time?" Marty quipped.

"Not for either of us. But we didn't exactly get a free ride either. Why don't you come in and I can tell you about it over a cup of coffee."

She waved for him to follow her on the walkway and up the porch steps into the house. Once inside she snapped on the lights and aimed for the kitchen.

"You know the drill," she called out. "Any seat with room." She peeked around the kitchen archway and saw Marty drape his jacket over the back of the recliner and sit down.

She fumbled in the cupboard for the coffee and scooped one spoonful into the coffee filter and then another onto the countertop. She tried to steady her racing heartbeat. This was silly, she thought. She was thirty-five years old and getting older by the minute. She should be able to handle male company, but this one made her feel different.

Unthinking, she brushed her fingertips across her lips remembering his kiss. He'd been affecting her composure every time she thought about him over the past few days, and if the jitters in her stomach meant anything, today would be no exception.

She finished with the coffee and then dropped a few chocolate chip cookies onto a plate. "Coffee's going to take a few minutes," she said, sliding the plate onto an end table.

She looked up and caught Marty's smile full force. It sent her stomach into cartwheels. The room seemed to be lit by the light of his smile and not from the sixty-watt bulb burning in the light she'd switched on when they came in. The way he looked at her made her feel like she had just touched a high-tension wire. And that was dangerous.

She walked around the room and turned on the lights, *all* the lights. She couldn't have him thinking that she invited him in to set up some cozy, romantic moment. Tempting as it seemed, she didn't want her mind wandering down that road either.

Soon the room glared as bright as the morning sun and there were no more lights to turn on. Satisfied, she curled up on the couch across from him and reached for a cookie hoping it would settle her vaulting nerves. It wasn't that she never had a man over before. It was just that this man was . . . well, different.

Marty had leaned forward with his forearms on his thighs and looked like a man tuned and ready. His hair was tousled and curled softly down into his shirt collar in the back. When he looked over at her through slightly hooded eyes, every female instinct in her screamed 'Bad Boy' and made every 'Good Girl' thought in her head fly out the window.

"So what was the sentence? Twenty-five to life?" he asked.

"Something like that. At least Mike thinks so. He agreed to community service starting this Saturday for about three hours and then every Saturday until he serves twenty-five hours."

"That's not so bad. What's he going to do?"

"The officer gave him a list of social service agencies that can use some help, but I don't think he's decided yet." She stood. "The coffee's probably done." She picked up the plate she'd set on the end table. "Cookie?"

"No thanks." Marty patted his stomach. "Ever since I left the NHL I find it much easier to pack on the pounds, what without the daily skates and drills."

"Nonsense." Stephanie stood as she replaced the plate on the table and then aimed for the kitchen. "I think you look great."

"Really?" Marty said with a tinge of satisfaction in his tone. "I didn't think you'd noticed."

Stephanie was glad she was in the kitchen as she felt her cheeks warm. "The poster on Mike's bedroom wall is one of you heading down the ice. I guess it's all that padding hockey players wear. You actually look thinner now." She grimaced, made a fist with her left hand and punched the air a few times. What in the world make her say that?

"Thanks, I think," he called back to her.

She returned with two mismatched mugs, a small glass of milk and some sugar packets on a black metal tray with red and gold flowers in the center. She moved a hassock closer and put the tray on it. "Mike knocked over the coffee table last week and broke one of the legs, so this has to do double duty these days."

"It's fine," Marty reassured, reaching over and taking the mug closest to him.

"I know you're probably used to inlaid cherry wood, or better yet, a maid serving coffee in bone china cups, but here it's ceramic on a foot rest.

"Really, it's fine. Why would you think that I would care anyway?"

Stephanie looked at him over the brim of her mug as she sipped. The blue sweater he wore bore the highly recognizable horse logo, and the watch that peeked out from under the cuff on his sleeve showed the silver circle of museum quality. His cologne smelled more like designer than drug store. "My colleague showed me the issue of *GQ* with you on it and in it. Some house you have there."

"I really only live on the first floor."

She set the mug down on the end table. "A swimming pool with a waterfall? Please. The only waterfall around here is the one on Mike's revolving light that he got from the new age shop at the mall."

"Maybe it is a little grandiose."

"Not for the Hills."

"You really need to stop by and let me take you on a tour. I'll prove to you that the place really is homey."

"With Mike's little escapade, I need to concentrate on him right now, not interior decoration."

"Can I help?"

"I worry about the time between school and when I get home. Idle hands as they say. I'd rather not give Mike the time and opportunity to go on another road trip."

"I know how I can help with that."

"How?"

"He can come by the rink right after school and do his homework in my office."

"Won't work."

"Why not?"

"Martin, Martin, Martin." She shook her head. "It hasn't been that long since you've been a teenager." She looked him up and down. "Well, maybe it has. But, trust me, he's not going to let you babysit him."

"Okay, so I'll hire him instead."

"To do what?"

"I have an open skating session about that time. He can help on the ice."

"Be a skate guard? I think he'd rather die than be caught dead in one of those jackets."

"He's fifteen, right?"

She nodded.

"He can't get behind a register in the pro shop, but he can help stock shelves, straighten out the hockey jerseys after the kids tear through them. Do you think he'd go for that?"

"What about his homework?"

"If he's swamped, he can pull up a corner in the snack shop and finish it before he starts work."

"Sounds good to me, but I already have a job. You'll have to ask Mike."

"Ask me what?" Mike walked in, squinting. "What the heck is going on in here. You could get sunburned from all this wattage." He turned off three of the lamps. "There. Now you don't need sun block." He dropped his backpack on the floor near the stairs. "Someone was going to ask me something?"

"I was." Marty walked to Mike and then hesitated. He hoped Mike wouldn't think that he was interfering. However, since he'd gotten to know the family, he discovered that he wouldn't really mind being the male figure in Mike's life for a while. In fact, he liked the idea of being the male figure in Stephanie's life too, but that might be harder to accomplish.

"Okay, what?" Mike responded when the silence got a bit awkward.

"How would you like to work at the rink?"

"Why?"

It was such a quick direct question that it caught Marty off guard. "Because I could use the help."

"You have a stack of applications about two inches thick on the counter in the pro shop. You don't need me."

Marty turned toward Stephanie and mouthed "help me out here."

She stepped forward. "It was my brainchild. I thought it might be a good idea if you had something to do between the time you got out of school and the time I got home from work."

"I don't need a babysitter, so your conspiracy isn't going to work."

"That's not it at all," Stephanie assured.

"Yeah, right," Mike replied.

"Don't rule it out so fast," Marty said. "CDs cost money, right?"

Mike looked at him. "Maybe it's a good idea." He started to bound up the stairs to his room. "I have a game in an hour and right now all I can think about is winning the opening faceoff."

Stephanie put her hand on the banister and leaned onto

the railing. "I think your working at the rink might take a few days off your grounding." She turned toward Marty. "Part of his at-home sentence."

Mike appeared at the top of the steps, hockey bag and stick in hand. "Sounds like a good compromise. After the game we can talk, okay?"

Stephanie smiled as she watched him take the steps two at a time and plunk the long, black bag in front of the door. "Plan on it."

He stood his hockey stick on end and picked at some loose tape on the curve of the shaft. "Okay then, let's go. I need to get my skates sharpened before the game." An impish smile curled his mouth. "Unless you want me to drive?"

"Oooh, no." Stephanie turned and started for the car keys that hung on a decorative hook in the kitchen. "You're most likely on the town's Ten Most Wanted list."

Marty pulled his keys from his jacket pocket. "Let me drive. We can talk a little about the job on the way. Okay?"

Mike picked up his equipment bag. "Sure, why not." He hiked the bag up onto his shoulder. "I'll call you when the game's over."

"Aren't you coming?" Marty asked Stephanie as he opened the front door and let Mike precede him.

"Some other time," Stephanie replied, holding open the front door as Marty stepped out. "We're having a staff meeting in the morning and I need to brainstorm some leads. Work's a little slow right now with not a supermarket opening in sight.

"If you change your mind, come up."

She nodded. "I will."

Chapter Six

This was very different from brainstorming ad ideas, Stephanie thought as she stood at the far side of the rink leaning on the railing in front of the bleachers over-looking the ice. Mike's team was leading 2–1. She caught sight of his number, eleven, as he sped down the ice on offense, protecting the puck and neatly dodging the pursuit of the opposing players.

When he took a shot from the left side, there was no light to tell the people in the stands that the goalie hadn't reacted quickly enough, no announcer to shout "and he scores," only cheers from parents and friends watching to tell the puck landed at the back of the net.

She watched him accept the glove-to-glove tap of con-gratulations from his teammates as he skated to the bench while another line prepared to fight for the puck at the faceoff at center ice. She felt pride but also a sense of regret that weighed down on her. Although she had been able to get to a few of Mike's games, this was the first time she'd seen him score.

She blew into the center of her cupped hands to warm them. She had forgotten about how cold it could be inside the rink. Woefully dressed for the occasion—other parents wore heavier coats, some even mittens to keep them warm—she had on a mid-weight jean jacket and hadn't even thought to take her gloves out of the bottom drawer in the dresser.

She blew again on her hands and smiled benignly at a hockey dad who had just finished yelling at the official. She watched the man nod at his son as the boy skated to the penalty box to serve a two-minute minor for tripping.

"Bad call," he said in response to her glance. "The kids just got tangled up going for puck."

"Uh-hum," she replied, worrying more about becoming a human Popsicle than about one team playing shorthanded. She turned back to watch the play resume when a hot cup of coffee seemed to appear in front of her eyes. She followed the attached hand and arm to a familiar face.

"You look like you could use this," Marty offered.

She took it eagerly and held it with both hands, feeling the warmth spread up her arm. "You are my hero. This might help me defrost."

"It's about 30 degrees in here. You need a scarf."

Stephanie took a long sip and felt the warmth extend down into her stomach. "And some long johns."

"The game *is* played on ice. Aren't you supposed to be studying for some kind of meeting?"

She laughed. "I got distracted." A few of the players crashed into the boards, drawing her attention to the rink in time to see Mike and another of his teammates scrambling back to their feet and skating furiously to catch up to the play. "Ouch. I wonder if I sounded like that when I fell."

"Probably not," Marty replied. "Those guys are pretty well padded."

A loud cheer went up from the crowd as the opposing team scored. Mike threw his stick into the players' bench area, hurdled the boards, and dropped into his place on the line.

"I'll be hearing about that one for the rest of the night when Mike gets home," Stephanie said. She watched Mike animatedly discussing the missed assignment with his coach.

"C'mon," Marty said, taking Stephanie by the elbow and gently steering her toward the steps. "Your nose is red. You need to warm up."

Stephanie transferred her coffee to one hand and covered her nose with the other. It felt like an ice cube. "But the game isn't over."

"There's less than a minute to play and the score is 3–2. I'm sure Mike's team will go into a defensive posture and hold the edge."

"Where are we going?" she asked descending the steps.

"My office. It's warmer and with no danger of frostbite."

"Hey Thomas." A teammate of Mike's sitting next to him on the bench elbowed him, and nodded toward the stands. "Isn't that your mom leaving with St. Claire?"

Mike looked up from the skate lace he had been tying in time to see Marty holding the door to the rink open as Stephanie walked through it. "Yeah," he shrugged. "So?"

"I thought your mom didn't like hockey."

"She doesn't much, why?"

"What's she doing here then?"

Mike leveled an indignant glare at his friend. "She likes me, that's why."

Mike's teammate shoved him teasingly. "Yeah, I bet that's the reason."

Mike shoved him back. "What are you getting at?"

"I've been watching them for the last few minutes," his friend said at about the same time the coach signaled for Mike's line to get back out onto the ice. Mike and his friend vaulted the boards and began skating toward the offensive zone. "And I think she's here for St. Claire."

Mike didn't have time to respond. An opposing player with the puck was headed his way.

Stephanie stood at the large windows that made up a wall in Marty's office and overlooked the ice rink. She rubbed her hands together. "You're right, this is much better. I think I'm thawing."

Marty stood beside her. "Mike's number eleven, right?"

Stephanie nodded. "Why?"

"Watch," Marty offered, pointing to the skaters. "I can tell by his body language he's about to make up for missing the check and letting the opposing team score a few minutes ago."

"There's no goalie on the other side. Doesn't he have to watch the extra attacker."

"So you do know something about hockey."

"A little," Stephanie conceded, wrapping her arms around her mid-section. "We were watching the Devils game on Sunday night and Mike explained to me about pulling the goalie. Sometimes it works for the team."

"And sometimes it backfires." Marty pointed at the ice.

Stephanie looked down at the rink in time to see Mike make a nifty move and steal the puck from the stick of an opposing player. He slipped past the last defender and headed toward the empty net. One slap shot later, victory was sealed as Mike's team went up 4–2 with ten seconds left.

"Nice move," Marty acknowledged. "He's a good skater and can handle the stick pretty well."

"I should know that," Stephanie said, turning her back to the ice and facing Marty. "But I don't." She moved to the desk at the other side of the room and set down the coffee cup. "And it stinks."

Marty joined her. "Don't you think you're being a little hard on yourself? After all, you are a single mom."

"No excuse," Stephanie said, turning back to the glass. Over Marty's shoulder she could see the teams in two lines skating past each other for the traditional post-game congratulations. "His team won today, but I can't even tell you what their record is. I should do more with him."

"I'm sure you spend a lot of quality time with him."

"Really now, Dr. Phil." Marty grinned and quickly lowered his head trying to wipe the smile from his face with his right hand. "You missed a spot," Stephanie quipped.

"I meant, I know how hard it must be for you to provide for Mike, keep up with his grades at school, make sure he's hanging around with the right crowd, and still try to make time for yourself too. Remember, you weren't even supposed to be here tonight."

Stephanie watched Mike's team skate off the ice as she spoke. "I do need to land some clients for the PR firm, but I needed to be here with Mike more." Her chest heaved and she turned back to face Marty. "I don't know how he got so old in such a short amount of time."

Marty walked to his desk and sat down. "Time goes on no matter how much we try to stop it." He signaled for Stephanie to sit on the chair across from him. "It seems like just yesterday that I was a rookie in the NHL. Now I'm an old man as far as the league is concerned."

Stephanie laughed as she settled in opposite him. "Thirty-eight is hardly old."

"Good guess."

"Not a guess," she corrected. "I read the article in *GQ*." She tipped her head. "I wish you would have told me about the house, estate, mansion, whatever you call it. I wouldn't have bothered you with a tour of my shack."

"It's not a shack. It's rather cozy. Actually, it reminds me of home."

Stephanie crossed her legs and rested her forearm on her knee. "Where's home?"

"Montreal. I live in the outskirts, but it's a beautiful city. You should see it sometime."

"Maybe I will."

"Now that's two places you've promised to check out," he reminded her. He hesitated momentarily then made the decision to take a chance. "I have an idea how you can cross one of them from your list rather quickly."

She straightened and folded her arms across her chest. "Do you now?"

"Yes. Come on up and see the house." He leaned forward and rested his elbows on the edge of the desk.

"Then you can see the velvet Elvis I was telling you about."

"Don't you have a supermodel tucked away up there somewhere?"

"I did once, but I'm currently available. Interested?"

Stephanie didn't need to hear any more. "It won't work."

"Of course it will. You just have to think positive."

"I know it positively won't work."

"Why not?"

"Because I don't date."

"Why not?"

"Job, child, trying to keep the house from being reported to the Board of Health in my spare time. Pick one. They all take a lot of work and occupy every minute of the day."

He flashed her a hopeful smile. "But you need time to relax. What about your sanity?"

She began to walk to the door. "If I'm counting right, sanity has dropped to about fifth or sixth place on the priority list right now."

Marty followed her slowly to the door. This one was going to be a challenge. Usually by this time he'd have had a date pinned down, be thinking about what wine to serve, be mentally picking out soft music for the CD player, and fantasizing about how the evening might end. But he was nowhere near any of that with Stephanie.

"Thanks for the invite, though," she added.

"Think about it." She started to say something, but he quickly continued. "Don't tell me now. Take a few days. I'll call you on Wednesday." He put his hand on the small of her back to escort her out the door and was jolted by a rush of something that felt like electricity moving up his arm when he touched her. The sensation seemed to find his heart and set it beating somewhere in the tachycardia range.

She turned to face him, her gaze rising to meet his. She looked at him as though she could see everything that was happening inside his soul. Almost without thinking, he took a step closer to her. Then another. The air between them crackled with expectation.

Just as he was about to act on his gut feeling to kiss her, his commonsense kicked in bringing him to a halt. This wasn't just any woman he wanted to kiss. It was Stephanie Thomas. The woman who fell on his ice, put peas on her leg, and cared more about family than about career.

The woman he thought didn't exist. The woman who was perfect for him.

Now that he'd found her, he didn't know quite what to do with her. He'd been kissing her a lot lately. Although he sensed she had enjoyed the kisses as much as he had, he knew he shouldn't pressure her so much. He needed to think long and hard about how to win her trust and her love before he assumed she would just melt into his arms. She didn't know him very well or very long, and he didn't want to scare her away by being too aggressive.

He stepped back, careful to put some distance between them. "Wednesday," he repeated. "I'll call you then. Hopefully, you'll have changed your mind."

Mike hoisted his hockey bag into the trunk of the Mustang. "Mom, can I ask you something?"

"Sure, ask away."

He slammed the trunk shut and bounced his hands on

top to make sure it was closed. "Is there something going on between you and St. Claire?"

"No," she said quickly, and then felt the heat from a blush rise on her cheeks from thinking about how he almost kissed her not five minutes earlier. "Why?"

"One of the guys on the team thinks there might be."

"Where would he get that idea?" she asked walking to the driver's side door and opening it.

"Newman saw you talking to St. Claire in the stands."

"That's harmless enough."

"I know, but if I do start to work here, between that and the community service I have to do for the stupid stunt I pulled, I don't need the ribbing."

"Your friend is wrong, honey," Stephanie assured. "I don't think I did anything to give anyone the impression that there is anything going on between Mr. St. Claire and me. We're just friends."

"I guess," Mike acknowledged, getting in on the passenger's side. "Maybe Newman is trying to get inside my head and mess with my game."

"Uh-huh," Stephanie replied, pulling the car door shut and starting the engine. "I bet that's all it is."

But even as she spoke as she pulled away from the curb, those funny feelings ran rampant through her body again. Maybe Mike's friend wasn't the only one getting inside someone's head.

Chapter Seven

Stephanie sat at her desk in her office tapping the well-used eraser end of a pencil against her chin. Her son's question at the hockey rink still nagged at her.

Did she have something going with Martin St. Claire? She'd said no, but just before she answered him, she felt an uncontrollable rush of sensations sweep through her— a quick elevation of her body temperature, tiny ripples settling in her stomach, a rise in her heartbeat.

They were the same physiological signs Officer Livak told her that lie detectors sense during the questioning of suspects. A long-time fan of police dramas on TV, she'd always been intrigued about how they seemed to always crack the case. She had asked Officer Livak about lie detectors while at the station dealing with her son. Thinking back again to the question, she felt sure that if she had been hooked up to one right now, the wire would not have only drawn loopy lines across the graph paper, but the ink probably would have squirted onto the wall.

Maybe it would be nice to have a relationship with a

man like Marty, but logically and for her, there was no way anything like that could happen. She was a single woman eking out a living for herself and her son, while he was a magazine cover-smiling, supermodel-dating, house-in-the-Hills-living celebrity. You couldn't get on much more opposite ends of the lifestyle and earning curve.

Besides, moments before she left his office that day, she thought he was going to kiss her, but he didn't. He plainly stopped himself. That had to mean something. The pencil tapping went even faster. Maybe he didn't consider her attractive. Maybe he didn't think there was any chemistry between them, which, of course, there wasn't, she assured herself.

The tapping slowed now. The lie detector would have registered another one. She did feel something, something that became stronger each time she saw him, but she didn't dare act on it. They were so different in so many ways. And there was Mike.

She sighed and let the pencil fall onto the desk. Watching it roll across the blotter, she concluded that it didn't appear as though this Cinderella would be going to the ball with Prince Charming anytime soon. She grabbed the pencil before it rolled onto the floor and began tapping it on her chin again. Looks like she would be back to kissing frogs and hoping for the best.

Tina walked into the office and plopped the morning's mail on the desk. "You have graphite on your chin, Steph." Stephanie continued to drum on her face like a member of a marching band. "Stressed about something?" Tina asked.

"No." Stephanie dropped the pencil into the center desk drawer and reached for the compact she had stashed there. She clicked it open, dipped her head and then rubbed her chin with her forefinger. Straightening, she held the mirror higher and studied her face. "Tina, am I a beast or something?"

Tina snorted. "A beast? What brought that on?"

Stephanie moved her head around to see all of her face, and preened, dabbing at her eye makeup and fluffing her hair. "Maybe I could use some highlights." She looked at Tina. "What do you think?"

"You look fine. What's up?" Tina asked, leaning a hip onto the door.

"I think I need a makeover."

"I'll rush out and call Ricki Lake."

"No, seriously." Stephanie put the mirror back in the drawer. "How do you think I'd look in short hair?" She gathered her hair into a ponytail with one hand. "Maybe a short, spiky style."

"It's not you."

"Maybe blond." Stephanie's eyes widened. "That's it, Barbie-doll blond with tanning-booth skin."

Tina made a disapproving face. "Why the sudden urge for change?"

Stephanie motioned for Tina to sit down as she spoke. "Remember I told you about Martin St. Claire?"

"You told me a lot. But besides from him being quite hunky, the only thing I remember worthwhile was that he kissed you." Tina saw the color rise on Stephanie's cheeks. "He kissed you again, didn't he? That's why you want your hair done into one of those new trendy styles. Am I right?"

"Not exactly."

"Then what?"

Stephanie slid back in the desk chair and looked at

the ceiling before looking back at Tina. "He almost kissed me again."

"Define almost."

Stephanie raised her hand, palm facing her eyes, fingers spread. "He was right here and then he . . ."

"He what?"

"Stopped."

"Stopped?"

Stephanie nodded. "Stopped."

'What do you mean stopped?"

Stephanie shrugged. "He just stopped. It was like he ran into a wall or something."

"Then why didn't you finish?" Tina asked casually, scooting forward in the chair and resting her forearms on the desk. "You wasted a perfectly good moment there."

"I couldn't do that."

"Why not?"

Stephanie had no answer.

"Hey," Tina continued, "how many moments do you expect to generate in the foreseeable future? It's not like you have a full dance card."

"I'm pretty busy," Stephanie protested.

"With who and when?" Tina challenged.

"Just last week I had a lunch date."

Tina laughed. "No you didn't. You shared a table at the bagel place with the FedEx guy because it was busy. That's not a date."

"Okay then," Stephanie said in triumph, "it was a moment."

Tina shook her head. "More like the Tuesday special." She sat back, laced her fingers together and rested her hands across her stomach. "I see that I need to intervene here."

"Tina," Stephanie's voice cautioned.

"Trust me."

Stephanie cocked her head in reservation.

"You said he asked you to come up and see his house, right?"

"Yes." The misgiving in Stephanie's tone deepened.

"Go do it."

Stephanie narrowed her eyes and pushed back in her chair. "I can't."

"That's the second time in five minutes you told me you couldn't do something. That's not you, Steph. You always told me you can do anything. Why not this?"

"Time," Stephanie replied. She angled her watch to her face. "It's two in the afternoon and I have three hours left to work."

"You haven't had lunch and you worked late last week. The place owes you some time." Tina reached over and grabbed a handful of brochures from the book-case next to Stephanie's desk. "Here, take these. Tell St. Claire you'd like him to give them to his friends or something."

Stephanie took them from Tina's outstretched hand. She looked from the company logo to Tina's eyes. "I suppose I could take the Reitman proofs to the graphics artist in Far Hills and swing by Martin's place on the way back." She smiled. "He did ask me to come over some time."

Tina stood, nodding. "And there's no time like the present."

"He might not even be there. He might be at the ice rink."

"I'll find out," Tina volunteered. She grabbed the phone. Stephanie didn't stop her.

As she watched Tina first get the number from information and then dial, Stephanie felt a rush of warmth flutter through her like she was doing something mischievous and might get caught. Truth was, the more she thought about it, the more she really did want to go see Marty's velvet Elvis.

"Okay," Tina said hanging up. "He's at the estate for the afternoon." She pulled Stephanie to standing. "He's all yours."

Chapter Eight

Stephanie stopped her car at the entrance to the driveway leading to Martin's home. She took a quick look in the rearview mirror, tempted to back out and drive off before anyone saw her. A silly notion, she decided before squaring her shoulders and going on.

The driveway arched around large trees and seemed to go on forever. She briefly wondered if she had the correct address right before the wooded area abruptly opened up to a finely landscaped section surrounding a beautiful house.

It was like nothing she'd ever seen before. A blend of wood, glass and stone, the front door looked as though it could have once graced an English castle. On either side were stained glass windows as tall as the door, but twice as wide.

The driveway disappeared behind the house, but she didn't follow it, choosing instead to park near the door. She grabbed the brochures and got out, in awe of the picture the place made. It looked as though it belonged on a postcard from somewhere in Europe.

She advanced up the ornately patterned brick walkway turning in circles as she did, not wanting to miss a single thing. She became so entranced in the scenery that she didn't hear the voices until she got closer to the front door.

Laughter and music drifted around the corner of the house. She retraced her steps and found that the walkway split. She followed the bricked path to the right like Dorothy going to Oz, and stopped dead in her tracks when she turned the corner at the back.

Women in lingerie were everywhere.

Her mouth opened. She felt as though her chin had dropped almost to the ground and she looked down to make sure it hadn't. Her instincts had definitely failed her and she felt extremely brainless. By the number of women scattered around the pool, Marty apparently had his pick of the litter and had picked them all. He certainly didn't need the likes of her around.

She turned quickly, intending to walk as fast as she could the way she had come and get out before anyone saw her. Instead, she barreled right into Marty, absorbing the solidity of his warm body and catching herself on his arms for a moment before releasing him.

"What a surprise," he said, smiling. "To what do I owe the pleasure?"

Stephanie dropped the brochures as she pushed away from him. As they both stooped to pick up the pamphlets, their heads clunked together with a soft thump. She tried to rub away the pain with the fingertips of one hand as she accepted the pamphlets from him with the other.

"I was delivering proofs to our graphic artist up the road and I thought I'd take you up on your offer to see the Elvis, but you're obviously busy." She stared around him but he stopped her with hands to her shoulders.

"I'm not busy," he countered. A feminine laugh rose behind him.

Stephanie stepped back. She pointed over his shoulder. "I think they would say otherwise."

"It's not what you think."

"It doesn't matter what I think."

He spun her around and gently urged her to walk the three steps to the back of the house. "They're not mine. Look closely at the pool near the waterfall."

She craned her head forward. She hadn't noticed the lights and equipment. "Cameras?"

"With photographers. It's a photo shoot."

Stephanie grimaced. "Then for sure I don't belong here. I should leave."

"Stay. I'll show you the house."

His smile shone brighter than the studio lights. She found it hard to refuse. "I don't want to be in the way."

"We won't be. They're losing the light and should be packing up any minute now. C'mon, let the professionals have the backyard." He took her elbow and guided her around front.

They walked together, brushing the occasional thigh and correcting the distance between them when they did. Stephanie's hand hit his as they turned the corner and she smiled an apology.

"Everyone says I walk in a zigzag pattern," she explained. "Most people give me plenty of room."

Marty moved his hand to the small of her back as they approached the front steps. "I'll take my chances." At the landing, he stepped to one side and bowed slightly at the waist. "After you."

Stephanie ran her hand across the finish of the ornately carved door. "This is beautiful. When I first saw it, I thought it belonged on an English castle."

"Funny you should mention that," Marty said, reaching up over the very high door to retrieve a key. "It did." He swept the door open and stepped aside, allowing her to enter first. "I found it in an antique store in London and had it shipped here after I bought the house."

Some house, Stephanie thought as she turned in a small circle in the entrance hall. *I think you could fit two of mine in here.*

"What are you thinking?" he asked in response to the look on her face.

Stephanie gave her head a tiny shake. "You keep a key in a crevice on top of the door?"

He shrugged and tossed the key into a modern art bowl with swirling colors of blue, green and purple that sat on a table just inside the doorway. "A throwback from having a working mother. Follow me. I'll give you the two-dollar tour."

She looked beyond him into a room that was a crazy mismatch of furniture and interior decoration. Distinctly masculine, nothing inside appeared to be decorator chic. An overstuffed sofa sat squarely in the center. Flanked by a recliner and what looked like a baroque dining room chair, it faced a small television set on top of a modern oak table.

"You did this yourself?" she asked.

"You don't like it?"

"It's okay."

"You sound like you just ate something awful and you

don't want to tell the cook." His voice was neutral, sounding neither proud of the décor nor embarrassed by it.

"No, it's wonderful, actually." She turned in even more circles as she followed him through a small hallway and stepped down into a large living room. "I pictured something more structured, that's all."

"The rest of the house was done by a decorator. This room is mine."

Stephanie took it all in. The walls there were made of stained wood covered with large oil paintings and wall hangings in shades of brown and tan with the occasional splash of complimenting colors. Bookcases jammed with books lined one wall. Several cases filled with plaques, trophies, and items that met sports milestones stood in front of another.

She walked to one and leaned forward. "Three-hundredth career goal," she said reading the inscription on one. She took a step to the right and scanned the many-framed pictures of Marty that indicated additional high points in his career. "Impressive."

"An aging sports star's memories," he explained with an almost embarrassed laugh.

"Aging?"

"A thirty-eight-year-old hockey player is normally ready for a rocking chair."

"You don't look any worse for the wear to me," she replied, sweeping his frame with her gaze.

"I'll take that as a compliment, but I'm sure I can find something better for you to look at."

"Like this," Stephanie said pointing to a third case. "2003 Man of the Year, United Way, Somerset Chapter." She pointed to another. "Care For Kids, 2003 Gold Award." She spun to face him. She nodded her approval.

Marty looked down and then quickly back at her. "You have to give something back."

As if on cue, light filtered in through crescent windows next to the fireplace and mixed with the sunlight coming in from windows on the far wall. It bounced off the glass of the trophy cabinets and lit the room, falling on Marty like a spotlight coming around to center on a star.

"Nice touch," she quipped. "All you need is a drum roll."

"I make sure that happens every time I bring someone in here."

He smiled at her and it nearly melted her heart. She wondered briefly if he knew how devastating that grin of his was to a woman's defenses. A lethal combination of looks, personality, success and generosity, she became acutely aware that Marty could find a permanent place inside her head and her heart if she wasn't careful. It was a normal reaction to a handsome man bathed in light that makes him look like an angel, she told herself.

Her gaze rose to meet his and something stirred inside her again. She did not waver. She looked into his eyes and felt as though she could see his soul. Almost without thought she took a step closer to him. She took in a deep breath and heard Marty's own breathing catch. Before she stopped to think, she leaned forward and touched her lips to his. His arm curled around her waist and she deepened the kiss as his other arm wrapped around her shoulders.

It was then that her mind went into a curious form of doublespeak and she was powerless to stop it. Instead of enjoying the wonderful kiss she had initiated, she began to wonder how she felt to him now that she was in his arms. She wasn't thin and lean like the women prancing around in lacy lingerie right outside the window. Round and curvy, she wondered if she felt, maybe . . .

Squishy.

The thought doused her enthusiasm like a bucket of cold water. She broke the kiss, her heart screaming in protest to the action her body was taking by stepping back. She blinked up at him. His lips looked so inviting that she could hardly stand it. Somehow she managed to think logically again.

"I should go," she said.

"Then that was some good-bye kiss," he said hoarsely.

She nodded. "And that's precisely why I need to get back to the office."

"But you haven't seen the Elvis yet," Marty protested. "It's in here in the office."

He started to walk toward an even larger room off to the right when a tall blond dressed in an ecru-colored teddy covered with a Belgian lace matching robe and carrying a champagne glass came into the room. "Martin, Carlos would like to see you before we leave. I think he wants to use the inside of the estate for a few shots." She walked to Stephanie, looking her up and down as she approached. "I don't believe we've met. I'm Kaylee. Kaylee McReynolds."

Stephanie felt her eyes widen with recognition. "The model. I bought one of those Angel Wings sets from Victoria's Secret because of the way it looked on you."

Kaylee grinned and took a final sip of the champagne. "Did you now?" She turned to Marty and held out the glass. "Could you be a dear and take this with you on your way outside?"

Marty took the glass and set it down on the oak end table. "Can it wait, Kaylee?"

"I don't think so. The shoot is on deadline."

He turned to Stephanie. "Wait here. I'll be right back." He quickly left and, in a few seconds, Stephanie could see him walking through the tall grass toward the pool.

Kaylee crossed her arms over her chest. "Are you a friend of Martin's?" Shifting her position, she cocked her hip to the right, the movement exposing a long expanse of slender thigh.

This lady is gorgeous, Stephanie thought. Tiffany's designer chic compared to her own style of TV Shopping Network affordable. Feeling quite uncomfortable, Stephanie began backing out of the room. "My son plays hockey at the ice rink."

"A business acquaintance then?" Kaylee matched her stride for stride, her expertly polished and manicured fingers drumming edgily on her upper arms.

"You could say that," Stephanie agreed. One more stride backward and her heel hit the step that she should have walked up to get out of the room. She teetered slightly before regaining her balance noticing that Kaylee did not even try to steady her. She rose onto the step and stood eye to eye with Kaylee. She was a tall one too, Stephanie thought. Tall, thin and beautiful. "Are you a friend?" She grimaced. Why did she ask that? She really didn't want to know.

A wry smile curled on Kaylee's perfectly lined, fashionably colored red lips. "Marty and I are more than friends," she said in a voice that almost purred. She slipped the robe from her shoulders. The material pooled at her elbows, exposing perfect shoulders.

"Thought so," Stephanie said, sprinting to the front door. There, she turned back to face Kaylee. "Nice underwear, by the way," she said right before she yanked it open, "if you need some dental floss," she added right before she closed it on Kaylee's stunned face.

"Where did Stephanie go?" Marty asked when he returned.

Kaylee used both hands to lift the hair from her shoulders. Then letting it fall, she shook her head so the sun-streaked blond strands moved around her face like wind blowing flower petals.

"She left," Kaylee answered. She walked to Marty and wrapped her arms around his neck. Eye to eye, she angled her head in an invitation. "There's some champagne and strawberries left. It can be just like old times." She didn't have to rise up to kiss him.

Marty gently pushed her away. "Kaylee, not now."

Not used to being dismissed, the diva in Kaylee kicked in. She threw her hands on her hips and pressed her lips together in a pique. "There are a hundred men I could think of that would kill for a moment like this."

"I'm not on that list anymore, Kaylee."

Her eyes narrowed. "I'm sure when you think about it, you'll regret that decision."

Marty watched her storm off and shook his head. "No, I won't."

Chapter Nine

"Stephanie, when you're in a hole, you're supposed to stop digging." Tina rested her backside on the edge of the old, blue kitchen table in the copy room at the office and took a sip of hot coffee from the mug in her hand. She set the mug down on the desktop and shook her head. "I like your underwear. Girl, what *were* you thinking?"

"I was thinking that the woman was a consummate snob and needed to be taken down a peg," Stephanie said, dropping her chin.

"And you felt compelled to use that particular moment to do it?"

Stephanie sighed. "I bet she thinks I'm a doofus."

"Haven't heard that word in a while. Conjures up a pretty nasty visual."

"Shouldn't you be out front typing something?" Stephanie poured the last bit of coffee left in the coffee maker into a Styrofoam cup. She added some milk from the small refrigerator under the table until it turned a light tan.

"Cranky, aren't we?" Tina asked.

"I didn't get much sleep last night."

"I guess not." Tina raised her mug in a salute. "Exchanging pleasantries with a supermodel in her underwear and kissing a sports hunk, all in the same afternoon. Quite a lot to ponder through the night."

Stephanie plopped the foam cup on the table and dropped into the well-used wooden chair near the window. "It's all your fault. You told me to make a moment." She raised her hands and eyes to the ceiling. "I made a moment."

Tina laughed and nearly spit out the coffee she had been drinking. She wiped a trailing drop from her chin with the back of her hand. "Forgetting the first and concentrating on the second, how did it go?"

Stephanie raised her eyebrows up and down a few times. "Pretty well I think."

"Good kiss?"

"*Great* kiss."

"Then who cares what a skinny blond in designer shorts thinks?"

Stephanie shrugged her answer.

Tina grinned and held out her mug. "Let's toast then. To moments."

Stephanie picked up her foam cup and held it high. "To moments," she repeated. "May there be more." Against her will, she felt her smile widen. "A whole lot more."

Marty wandered over to the window in the conference room of the Coreman Group and stared out. He had no idea if he was doing the right thing, but hoped Stephanie would see the gesture he was about to make as thoughtful. However, he conceded, she could also think of it as patronizing.

Years ago he faced the reality that most women were attracted to him because of his star status. He learned to listen to his instincts when he met them, careful to not let himself be caught up in thinking any of them had wanted to meet him, and get to know him for the man inside.

Then Stephanie came into his life. She was different. He stuffed his hands into his pants pockets and, thinking back to the day she put frozen peas on her ankle, laughed. It was a genuine action for her. No other woman he'd ever dated would have lowered her façade that much in his company.

He tried to picture Kaylee doing something open like that and laughed harder. Kaylee would have been camped out at an orthopedist, dabbing at her artistically lined and mascaraed eyes, wailing about not being able to glide down the catwalk in four-inch stiletto heels. She would have made sure her face, wracked with staged pain and concern, accented her story, which would make the front page of every entertainment and fashion magazine in existence.

He shook his head. Fur-clad movie stars and uppercrust somebodies on his arm were fun, for a while. But the parties, the front-row, center-stage tickets, and luxury suite treatment hadn't quite become as comfortable for him as he had been assured they would become.

Worth doing? Yes, as long as he put in perspective what the hero worship really was; only there for the asking as long as he stayed a hot commodity.

Worth trying to hold onto for the rest of his life? No, if it meant not being able to sit in the cheap seats once in a while with someone he cared about without some reporter asking him why.

He put all the emotional matters on hold, away from his heart and conscience when he made it big, and had concentrated on the rewards. But meeting Stephanie reminded him of what was important and real. Sometimes he could hardly believe she had made such an impact on his life. Since he had met her, he didn't want to be in *GQ* with someone like Kaylee anymore. He wanted to be in *Family Circle* with Stephanie. But could he convince her that he meant it after knowing her for only a few weeks? The run-in with Kaylee surely wouldn't help his case.

He understood completely why Stephanie left the estate in such a hurry that day. He dropped his head and let out an audible breath. Kaylee McReynolds in her underwear, looking down her pert nose could scare most women away.

He turned from the window at the familiar sound of Stephanie's voice and put his soul searching on hold. He called to her as she walked by the door to the conference room.

"What are you doing here?" she asked, stepping inside.

"I called, but you were out to lunch, so I took a chance and came down without an appointment. I hope that's okay."

"Sure. Sure it is."

Marty's gaze swept her head to toe and she strode in from the hall, her hair swinging, her smile shaped by a soft shade of pink lipstick that accented the surprise he saw in her eyes. The subtle scent of perfume surrounding her was meant for a man to remember. Her business suit wasn't overly short, just enough to draw his attention to her legs. He stared at the curve of her calf and taper of her ankle. She had great legs. He felt his smile widen just as he heard her say his name again.

"Marty, are you feeling all right? You look a little strange."

Before Marty had a chance to answer her, Richard Coreman joined them. "Stephanie you're back. Good." He pointed down the hall toward his office. "Let's seal this deal right now." As he passed Stephanie on his way out of the conference room, he whispered, "Nice work signing St. Claire."

Stephanie's mouth fell open. "What do you mean?" She called after him as he made his way down the hall with Marty. "Signed him to what?" Marty turned and smiled weakly at her. In two long strides, Stephanie was beside him. "What have you done?"

Marty felt a small surge of caution run through him. He definitely should have discussed this with Stephanie first. Acutely aware that the small hallway was rapidly ending, he raised his hands in a defensive posture.

She arched her brow. "Marty, what have you done?"

He cleared his throat, desperate to summon up the right words. There were none immediately available to him.

Chapter Ten

Later, at the coffee shop around the corner, Marty tried to make conversation. "You're angry." He leaned forward in the booth. "You haven't said a word since we left your office."

Stephanie dabbed at her mouth with a paper napkin and waited until a young fan got an autograph from him. "I'm fine. Coreman asks me to take our new client out to lunch, so I take him out to lunch. I always eat two lunches on Tuesdays."

"You *are* angry."

"You think?" Stephanie scooped up the check the instant the waitress brought it to the booth.

"I'll get that." Marty started to reach out, but abruptly changed his mind when Stephanie held up a finger in distinct warning.

"I can afford this," she said. "I have an expense account now thanks to you."

"That's a good thing, right?"

Stephanie stood, grabbed some money from her purse

and tucked a $4 tip between the salt and pepper shakers. "I can't take credit for your signing with the agency. I have to go back and tell Coreman I had no idea what you were planning on doing."

Marty looked sheepish. "I probably should have discussed it with you first."

"Okay, I admit, I need new clients, but I'd rather find them on my own. It may take a few more days or weeks than I would like, but I like doing things on my own."

"You will," Marty assured. "Any ad campaign for the rink will be your brainchild. I am definitely not creative."

Stephanie sighed and looked down at her napkin. "That's not it." She lifted her head and looked into his eyes. "Simply, I need to know I can count on myself to be successful. It's important to me."

"I just wanted to help you."

"Shouldn't have to make it with your help."

"We all need help one time or another," Marty countered.

"What kind of help does someone like you need?"

"The rink isn't exactly in the black. I could use some help attracting more business to keep it self-supporting. For that I could definitely use some help with the PR."

Stephanie laughed. "I don't think you need me for that. You're a big sports star."

"Ex-sports star," Marty corrected.

"With an estate and a supermodel girlfriend, who could probably call Donald Trump and get him to add stadium seating, a practice rink, and some laser tag to the arena."

"That's exactly what I had in mind," Marty said, pointing a finger at her.

Stephanie felt her brow crease. "Then call her." She rose. "I can't come close to that."

Marty pulled her back to sitting by the hem of her suit jacket. "I don't mean Kaylee, I mean the rest of the stuff you said."

"Hey," she protested, bouncing down onto the vinyl bench. "Watch the hands. No checking from behind." She settled back into the seat. "I don't quite understand. You could probably contract for the add-ons yourself. Your name alone should attract investors."

"Yes, but even superstars have to be careful about deals. Signing with the Coreman Agency is strictly a business move."

"Really?" Stephanie muttered.

"Yes, really."

"Don't you already have an agent or something?"

"For salary issues when I was in the NHL, I did. But when I retired, we parted company. I'm not one for going to memorabilia shows and sitting for three hours signing my rookie card so the card shops can sell it for a couple hundred dollars. If someone asks me when he or she sees me to sign something, fine, I'll do it. No one has to pay me for that. But . . ."

"I have a bad feeling about this."

"Don't. I would like someone to promote the rink and maybe help me attract an investor that will eventually take it over. I like the idea of offering the opportunity for more people to love skating the way I do, but eventually, I'd rather consult, maybe run a few clinics or help with some summer hockey camps. Hockey occupied all of my time and attention for the last fifteen years. It was intense, sometimes painful, and didn't give me much chance for enjoying a normal life. I really would like a more relaxed pace now. Owning a business doesn't often lend itself to that."

"You're right about that," Stephanie admitted. "But wouldn't a high-powered PR firm from New York be more your style?"

"Not necessarily. A New York firm doesn't know the local area. I'm not trying to attract Manhattan business-men to play in an over-forty league. I want kids to learn to love the ice. Maybe give a kid the chance to develop his skills . . ."

"Or her skills," Stephanie reminded.

"Or hers," Marty agreed, feeling a grim play on his lips, "enough for a coach to notice so he or she can get a full ride to college on a sports scholarship."

Stephanie gave him a brilliant smile. "Your logic is pretty hard to argue."

"Good," he said, trying to keep his focus. The way she looked at him was sending everything inside of him into high gear.

"Then you go back to the rink and start making a list of ideas while I hit the desk at the office and do the same."

He frowned. "Shouldn't that be something we do to-gether?"

"Not at first. We need to compare lists and see how close we come to thinking along the same lines."

Reluctantly he agreed. "I guess I could get more done if you weren't side-tracking me all afternoon."

"I can't possibly be that distracting."

"That's not exactly the word I'd use to describe you." He reached out one hand to brush the hair gently off her temple.

Stephanie's eyes softened even further with his touch. "Tell me."

"If I do, then you'll have to promise to meet me at the rink tonight."

Her eyes narrowed. "You don't play fair."

"I was among the players with the most penalty minutes during my last season."

She regarded him thoughtfully. "I suppose I can shake an hour or so free tonight after I make sure Mike has done his homework."

"It's settled then." He rose and extended his hand to her. "Eight o'clock then?"

"Sounds like a plan." At the register, she paid the bill, but paused by the glass door leading out of the small restaurant. "Wait a minute, you never told me the word."

Marty reached around her and pushed open the door, waiting until she went through before he did. "What word?"

As they began to walk in opposite directions, she made an impatient gesture with her hand. "The word you would use to describe me."

Marty turned around, walking backward so she could see him. "Oh, that word."

"Well?" she called out. "What is it?"

He winked at her just before he reached the municipal parking lot. "I'd say you are. . . perfect."

Her mouth fell open as he made a quick escape around the corner.

Mike looked up from rummaging through his hockey bag when Stephanie opened the front door.

"I'll need new skates soon," he announced, holding one up for her to see. "These are pretty beat up."

"Can you hold out for a few weeks?" Stephanie asked, tossing her purse in its usual spot between the sofa and the end table before heading to the kitchen. She heard Mike run up the stairs. "I think the car needs new tires," she called out as she opened the refrigerator and retrieved what was left of last night's dinner.

The sound of footsteps and the thump of what had to be a jump from the second or third step preceded Mike's voice. "I guess so."

"Did you eat? There's not much left of this chicken." Stephanie set the plate in the microwave and set the reheat timer for two minutes.

Mike appeared in the doorway, bag hoisted onto his shoulder, hockey stick in hand. "I have a game, remember?"

"Sorry, I didn't. But you should eat anyway."

"The coach usually gets us pizza after the game. I don't like to play with a full stomach in case I get checked hard."

Stephanie smiled. "Can't mess up the ice, can we? I forgot you had a game tonight." A car horn answered her. "Guess you have a ride there. Need one home? I'm—"

"No, got it covered. Later, Mom," Mike called out, already walking to the front door. "Gotta run. I have to get some of that community service done first."

". . . meeting Marty at the rink tonight," she finished as the door slammed behind him. "We're discussing business," she whispered.

She took off her suit jacket and began climbing the stairs to change. The meeting was business, not pleasure, she rationalized.

But she had to admit that soon she'd have to find a

real balance in the matter, which was becoming one more of heart than of work.

"Hey Mike!"

Mike turned toward the voice and saw Marty stepping out of the elevator in the lobby of the ice rink. He raised his chin and tossed his head, acknowledging Marty. "Hey," he replied.

"Have a game tonight?" Marty asked pointing to Mike's hockey bag.

"Yeah, eight o'clock. If we win, we can lock up a playoff spot." He shifted his weight to his other leg and settled the bag farther back on his shoulder.

"Aren't you a little early?"

"I'm working off some of the community service. The after school program at the Y is bringing some of the kids here to skate, and I have to help make sure no one goes the wrong way on the ice and messes up the other skaters."

"Are you almost done with that?"

"A couple more hours."

Marty took a step closer to Mike. "I'd like to talk to you for a few minutes, if you have the time."

Mike shook his head. "I don't really. The bus is already here. Can it wait?" He watched some of the muscles in Marty's face tense for a moment before they relaxed. "Am I in some kind of trouble?"

"No," Marty assured. "I'd like to talk to you about your mom."

Mike dropped his hockey bag. It hit the concrete floor with a dull thud. He draped his sticks across it. "Anything you want to know about my mom should come from her."

"It's not actually her I want to talk about."

"But you said—"

"I want to ask you something."

Mike shrugged. "Ask away."

"How would you feel if I asked your mom out on a date?"

The question hit Mike like a punch in the stomach. A date? His mom and St. Claire? It had always been just his mom and him, and he liked it that way. She was always there for him, always had his back. If someone else was in the mix, she might have to choose. He didn't like the way it made him feel just thinking about it.

"Why do you want to date my mom?" Mike asked as a stall.

"Because I like her."

"Why ask me then?"

"Because I know she would care what you'd think, and I respect that."

Mike picked up his sticks and slung his bag back over his shoulder. "Then I don't know if I want you to," he said as he turned away from Marty and headed for the blue rink.

Marty sat in his office mentally kicking himself. He had no experience dealing with teenagers. He shouldn't have broached the dating subject with Mike. It was too early. Everything inside his gut told him he should wait a while for that, but everything inside his heart had told him otherwise. He would have to wait and see just how much damage he'd done.

The sound of his office door opening made him look up from the doodles he had been making on the ledger paper on the desk. He looked up and saw Stephanie.

"You're early," he said dropping the pencil in his hand and glancing at his watch.

Stephanie pointed at the door behind her. "I can go, if you're busy. Maybe another time would be better."

She started to turn but Marty stood and held up his hand. "No, it's fine. I can wrap this up in about ten minutes, if you're willing to wait around for me." He sat back down and motioned to a chair alongside his desk. "It isn't very comfortable, but it's a place to sit."

"I got done a little sooner than I expected with home stuff," she said as she sat, crossing her legs and bouncing her foot in a visual display of nerves. "I hope I haven't interrupted something important."

"No," he replied with a swipe of his hand. "I'm just catching up on the week's reports. Stay." He held out a box of doughnuts. "Have dinner?"

Missed aerobic classes crossed her mind, but she took one anyway. "Yes, but not dessert."

Marty poured water from a pitcher on his desk into a paper cup and handed it to her. "I probably should have warned you that those were left over from this morning's breakfast."

"Sounds like a dinner staple in my house."

"You deserve something better than stale pastries. We can get something to eat, if you'd like?"

Stephanie refused with a small swipe of her hand. "I've had too much food and not enough exercise lately."

"I think I have a remedy for that."

"What, a magic pill that will shave some cellulite from my thighs in ten minutes?"

Marty glanced at her legs. "They look fine to me."

Stephanie stopped shaking her foot and surveyed his

eye-catching, fun-loving smile. "What would your girl-friend say if she heard you flirting with me?"

His smile turned up a notch. "What would your boy-friend say if he saw that you were enjoying it?"

"I don't have a boyfriend."

"And I don't have a girlfriend. That means we're both unattached. And while we're on the subject, sort of any-way, I think there's definitely something starting between us. An attraction, at least. Don't you agree?"

Caught offguard, Stephanie lifted an eyebrow. "Attraction?" She had to admit; he was appealing. "I like you," she confessed.

Marty nodded his reaction to the dodge. "Not exactly a grand declaration, but a starting point." He stood. "Back to the beginning of this drifting conversation. How's your ankle?"

Stephanie looked down. She flexed and extended her foot a few times. "It feels really good. I think I'm cured."

"Good." Marty walked around the desk and took her hand. "Then let's skate off the doughnut."

Stephanie furrowed her forehead. "I thought we were going to discuss business?"

"We can do that later. Carpe diem. Seize that day. We may not get another chance like this one."

"I noticed the parking lot was full and I know Mike said he had a game. Don't you have to make sure the rink is ready and the referees are on time?"

"Normally, but I hired a rink manager today. He can do all that. And although both rinks are being used, the practice rink is free in the back. Usually, one of the league teams is using it, but not tonight. It isn't very often that there's some free ice here." He tugged on her hand. "Come on, it'll be fun."

Stephanie looked up from her hand to Marty's eyes and wrinkled her nose.

"What?" he asked. "You look like you just ate a bug."

"Ever see *Rocky*?"

"Sure, who hasn't?"

"Remember the skating rink scene?"

Marty grinned. "Yes."

"Well, Adrienne skates better than I do."

"Are you ready?"

Stephanie looked out over the ice. The surface appeared as smooth as glass and the enclosed rink looked a lot bigger once you got on it than it did from the outside. She moved her finger in a circle. "You first."

Marty stepped onto the ice. Skating backward, he beckoned with both hands. "Yo, Adrienne. The doughnut, remember?" He skated back to her. "Come on out."

"Show me your stuff first." She shooed him away with a few quick swipes of her hand. "Go on. Dazzle me."

"If you insist."

He skated away from her with long, effortless strides, the lightweight jacket he wore fit nicely across his shoulders, and as he pushed forward in the power stroke of the glide, the jeans he wore accented the muscles of his thighs. Stephanie watched him intently. She was, after all, only human.

Marty looked back over his shoulder and caught her staring. In response he abruptly stopped, the edges of his skates producing a small snow squall of shaved ice that flew about three feet into the air.

She applauded as he moved smoothly back to her. "Very nice. Now do one of the Lutz jumps," she said when he was right in front of her. "What is a Lutz, any-way?"

"We don't Lutz in hockey," he reminded her. "We . . ." he smiled wide, ". . . body check."

Stephanie closed her eyes in mortification. His one-liners more than matched hers. "Don't get any ideas. This is one body that doesn't need checking," she said when she opened her eyes.

He held out his hand. "Your turn."

She could not think of any more diversions. She was trapped. Taking the hand he offered, she stuck the tip of one skate onto the ice. "You have no idea what you're asking. I trip over cracks in the sidewalk."

"There are no cracks to trip over here," he said. "The Zamboni just did its thing right before we came in."

Stephanie moved her shoulders in a sign of surrender. "Okay. But stay close." Her entire right skate was on the ice now. "Here I come." With hesitation in her body language, she moved fully onto the ice. She let out a long breath of air. "Now what?"

He took both her hands. "Try moving."

"I did that once and ended up on my rear."

"I won't let you fall."

"I'm going to hold you to that."

With something resembling a child taking its first steps, Stephanie moved forward, wobbling more than skating. Her feet moved in shuffle-like movements, making her look like she was scuffing her feet. About three feet away from the edge of the rink, she skidded, pitching forward right into Marty's arms.

"Yikes," she shouted, grabbing onto his upper arms for support. When she finally settled on her skates, she noticed Marty trying to suppress a laugh. "And I suppose you did better your first try?" she challenged.

"Probably not," he conceded. "I was two."

"If I wasn't so afraid to let go, I'd punch you in the arm."

"I'll remember that," Marty replied, settling her alongside him and slipping an arm around her waist. "Now lean on me and let me lead." He pulled her into an easy glide before she had a chance to say no.

He didn't tease her again when she pitched forward, and then to one side when they turned around to skate back after reaching the far end of the rink. He did keep an infuriating smile on his face as they moved smoothly along.

Stephanie ignored him as much as possible and tried to concentrate on lengthening her stride as she moved with him. Each time she reacted to a slip by holding onto him tighter, a rush of warmth coursed through her, the temperature in the rink doing nothing to help douse the heat.

Marty, meanwhile, maintained an athletic command over his body, gliding almost gracefully, while still being able to steady her on the ice. As they moved along the large oval surface, she had to consciously fight her female instincts to snuggle into the lines of his body. Her hormones went on a slow but steady drip, building and accumulating until she was aware of almost nothing else.

"Easy," he said as he caught her around the waist when she flailed, took a few slippery steps when she crossed her skates, and nearly fell.

"I'm okay," she said, steadying herself.

"You sure?" He didn't seem to be in a hurry to remove his hands.

"Yes." She shifted away from his hip.

Marty pulled her back. After a momentary resistance, he felt her relax. Careful to keep her steady, he reached out and traced the curve of her jaw. "Can I kiss you now and get it over with?"

Stephanie blinked. "Don't feel as though you have to."

"I don't. I want to." He stared at her for a long moment. "So can I?"

She saw anticipation in his eyes as he waited for her to say yes. A realistic assumption since every part of her body, including the small part of her brain that still functioned, wanted to move toward him and get closer. She could only imagine all the women over the years who had fallen under this same spell.

He pulled her gently closer. "Can I take the silence for a yes?" His smiled turned tender as his gaze moved from her eyes to her lips before he moved his mouth to hers, offering a slow and lingering kiss.

Sure the ice beneath her feet would melt at any moment, she resigned herself to cold feet and wet socks and kissed him back. She looped her arms around his neck and leaned more fully into him for support.

She felt him grin against her lips as he began to slowly skate backward, pulling her with him while he continued to kiss her. It was the most incredible sensation she had ever experienced. Eyes closed, gliding, kissing, she became lost in the heaven that was the moment.

Out of the blue, the tone changed and it felt as though her brain was knocking on her heart. This shouldn't be happening. He was a client and definitely out of her league. Even though it felt so right, it was so wrong. But she didn't care. Not right now anyway. When he finally pulled back, she let her fingers slide away from his neck and onto his shoulders.

"Are you okay?" he asked.

"Why?"

"You have that bug look on your face again."

Actually, in a way, she felt better than she ever had in her life. An incredibly handsome, sought-after man had just kissed her. She felt alive with a beyond-words feeling inside her heart that overtook the sensible part of her brain and sent it packing.

"I'm just fine," she acknowledged. She couldn't stop the wide grin that curved her mouth.

He smirked. "The bug look is actually quite attractive on you."

Her arms slid back around his neck and she lost herself again in the sheer delight of his kisses.

Inside the locker room Mike was peeling the white tape from his ankles when a hockey glove went flying by his head and hit the concrete wall with a whap. When Mike looked in the direction from which it came, Joey stood by the door grinning from ear to ear.

"Hey, watch it," Mike said, tossing the glove back to him, "you could take an eye out with that."

"Pity," Joey replied crossing his arms over his chest. "Then you wouldn't be able to see what I just saw." He raised his eyebrows up and down a few times. "And I assure you that you want to see this."

"Cut it out, Joey. It's late and I'm tired. Before the game I had two hours of making sure the kids from the Y who were on the blue rink didn't do anything stupid." Mike stripped his hockey jersey from his body and began to undo the straps on his shoulder pads. "Two more hours and I'm done with the stupid community service that you and your joyriding idea got me sentenced to. My mom nearly killed me after that stunt you pulled."

"Quit whining." Joey admonished Mike with a disapproving glare. "It isn't community service that's going on outside, but it does involve your mom."

Mike stopped unlacing his skates and snapped up his head. "My mom's home."

"I don't think so," Joey replied in a singsong voice. "I think you'd better come with me."

Curious now, Mike secured the rubber guard to the blades of his skates and followed Joey.

Stopping just at the glass doors leading to the practice rink, Joey beckoned Mike closer. "Good, they're still there."

"Who is still where?" Mike asked.

Joey's smile turned nasty. "Your mom and St. Claire."

"Impossible," Mike challenged, moving closer to the doors. "My mom doesn't know how to skate, and besides, she's at ho—" He realized Joey was telling the truth. His mom stood in the middle of the practice rink, kissing St. Claire.

"There you go, my man," Joey chuckled, slapping Mike on the shoulder. "Looks like your mom and St. Claire are practicing the double lip lock." He snickered. "And I think the French judge will give them a perfect ten."

Chapter Eleven

"**Y**ou did well," Marty noted when they were back in his office on the second floor. He stored both pair of skates under his desk. "Are you cold? Would you like some hot chocolate? I think the snack bar is still open."

Stephanie looked at her watch and shook her head. "No, thanks. If Mike's game isn't over already, it probably will be soon. I should wait for him outside."

"Don't go yet," Marty suggested. "It's been a while since I had that much fun on skates, and I'd like to try to continue that feeling for a little while longer."

"It was nice."

"Just nice? I invented backward-skating kissing just for you!"

Stephanie chuckled. "Your style told me otherwise."

"No, honestly. It was a spontaneous move."

"You admit it was a move." She watched his face color with a blush. "But a very pleasant move," she added, letting him off the hook.

"Can you stay just for a minute or two?" Marty indicated the empty chair near his desk.

"A minute," she agreed, sitting.

He looked at her and slowly shook his head. "What is it? Is my timing off with the place you are in your life right now?"

"What do you mean?"

She knew. The pull that existed when they were together had gotten stronger. In her life, the times she regretted the most were the times she hesitated. One way or another, this would be settled tonight.

"Never mind. Don't answer that question," Stephanie cautioned.

Marty's eyes narrowed as he watched her walk around the desk toward him, and he turned in his chair as she approached. She didn't stop until her thigh hit his knees, the attraction surrounding them no longer as indistinct as it had been just moments before.

"Marty," she said resting her hands on his shoulders. Her gaze stayed on his face but focused on his lips.

"Yes?" His hand on the desk dropped the pencil he was holding.

For a while they stared at each other while sparks seemed to sizzle and zap the air between them. Then she leaned forward and kissed him, gently molding to him with gentle care.

He made a quiet sound in agreement and pulled her onto his lap. Her arms wrapped around his neck. Quivers started at the base of her spine and raced up her nerve-endings, making everything inside her tingle.

The taste of his lips was spicy, his mouth firm as it slanted against hers, taking control of the kiss. Stephanie started to feel lightheaded. He kissed her like a man who wanted her. Needing air, she freed herself and took a long, shuddering breath.

Marty's voice was low and breathless when he spoke. "What's going on here?"

"A kiss?"

"Just a kiss?"

"Or maybe more," she tested. "What do you want?"

"I could want a lot."

"So could I." She looked into his eyes and practically melted on the spot. It had been so long since anyone made her feel this way. Why shouldn't she want more of the same? "Maybe we should talk."

"In a minute," Marty said pulling her back to him.

Stephanie wrapped her arms back around his neck and let him kiss her again. Everything she was feeling inside seemed to wrap around her like a cozy fleece blanket and, for the moment, time stopped.

"Yep, I'll bet they're upstairs in his office making out on the desk," Joey announced as he picked up his hockey bag and slung it over his shoulder.

The statement caught the attention of a few of Mike's teammates. "Who's makin' out with who?" one of the boys asked, a devious smile racing across his face. "I saw Shelly from school in the stands earlier. Is it her?"

"Naw, someone better."

"Shut up, Joe," Mike warned. "It's nothing, Greg. You know Joey likes to exaggerate everything."

"This is no exaggeration," Joey countered. He tossed his head in a subtle challenge. "And you know it, Thomas."

"What? What?" Greg stopped packing his bag and scooted over next to Mike. "Spill it, what do you know?"

"Let it go, Greg."

Joey dropped his hockey bag back onto the locker room floor and walked over to the bench. "Sure you'd like us to let it go. Then you'd be on your way to locking up the captain's spot. Coach said it was a fight between you, me, and Greg, but I didn't think you'd bring in your mom as a reinforcement."

Greg furrowed his brow. "What the heck are you talking about, Joe?"

"Thomas, here," he cocked a thumb at Mike, "well we all know his game's been slipping lately." Joey kicked the corner of Mike's hockey bag with the toe of his sneaker. Mike didn't respond, only continuing to pack the bag. "I think he found a way to overcome his lack of talent and stay on the good side of the coach."

"Shut up, Joey," Mike warned. He zipped his bag and stood toe to toe with his friend. Staring Joe right in his eyes, he added, "If you know what's good for you."

Greg took a step back. "If this is on a need-to-know basis, man, maybe I don't need to know."

"Gonna find out sooner or later," Joe blatantly continued. "Might as well be from me."

"Joey, I'm warning you. Zip it. I don't have time to deal with this garbage right now."

"How gallant, riding to your mom's defense," Joey mocked, making like he was charging on a horse.

Mike's body language screamed his annoyance, and his face tightened. He held back from rushing Joey through sheer force of will alone.

"What does Mike's mom have to do with Shelly, and who is going to be captain of this team?" Greg asked, as the tone of the locker room changed from lighthearted to serious.

"You loser," Joey sniped. "Try to keep up, will you. Fact is, I saw Mike's mom lip-locking with St. Claire a few minutes ago on the practice rink."

Greg took two steps to the door. "This I gotta see."

"Don't bother," Joey said, "I saw them go up toward his office. Bet they're hot and heavy by now making sure Mike's captaincy is secure."

Laughter erupted from among the remaining members of Mike's team, accompanied by whistles and shouts. For Mike, it was the proverbial straw that broke the camel's back.

As if taken over by some unseen force, Mike's right hand shot out and caught Joey square in the nose. Joey countered by throwing himself at Mike, and together they fell to the cement floor of the locker room. A few punches were exchanged before their teammates pulled them apart.

"Quit it, guys," Greg warned, "or you'll both be suspended from the team."

Joey wiped the blood from his nose with the back of his hand. "Not him," he said, nodding toward Mike in a gesture that challenged. "Not teacher's pet."

Mike cupped his aching right eye. "Just shut up." He scooped his equipment and hockey bag and strode to the door with angry steps. Once there he paused. "You know, jerk, if there is anything going on between St. Claire and my mom, it's none of your business anyway, so shut your pie-hole." Feeling his comments needed no further explanation, he left.

As he walked out to the parking lot, Mike felt his chest tighten. He had a feeling, and now it was confirmed. His mother and St. Claire were together.

Remembering the conversation earlier, Mike felt be-

trayed. St. Claire really didn't care how he would feel
about his mom dating. It had been already set up. St.
Claire was just covering all the angles.

But his mom. Ever since St. Claire had come into her
life, she'd been acting all funny and stuff. She never
hung out at the rink before. Now she'd been here twice
in the last three days.

For years it had only been the two of them. She didn't
need anyone to look after her. That was his job, and he
didn't want or need any help doing it.

Cripes, he thought, as his stomach dropped. Just what
he needed. Why did he ever take her to skate with him
that day anyway?

Marty sat on the leather sofa in his office, Stephanie
next to him, his arm around her shoulders, her legs
tucked under her. Her eyes were closed and she was
smiling.

"What are you thinking about?" he asked, kissing her
forehead as he spoke.

She turned her head and buried her face in his shirt.
"I can't believe what a hussy I've turned into since I met
you," her muffled voice replied. She turned back and
settled into the curve of his arm. "You must think I'm
awful."

"Not at all." He eased her back. "Where did that word
hussy come from anyway? It sounds colonial or something." He laughed. "Hussy. It sounds like it should be
the description of something leaking air." He cocked his
head. "The tire got a hussy and went flat after ten
minutes."

Stephanie sat up and rested her elbow on the back of
the sofa laughing. "Hmm, interesting use. I like it.
Atypical, yet descriptive."

"Actually," he said, his tone turning serious, "I'm more interested in what might happen next."

"I guess we should talk."

"Or explain. I am really sorry about setting up the PR thing. I really should have consulted you first."

"I won't argue with the fact that the commission is going to be nice. I had been wondering how I was going to fit some much-needed repairs into the budget when you showed up. But I do feel like I'm deceiving the boss."

"Not to worry," he reassured, "I'm sure you're going to more than earn it." He saw her face suddenly darken and she looked down at the hand in her lap. "Something wrong?"

She glanced back up at him. "Have you ever wondered about that warning, be careful what you wish for?"

He shook his head. "I can't say that I have." He reached over and took her hand in his.

Stephanie bit down on her lower lip. "I never put any stock into that adage until now. I think I want to be with you, but I know I shouldn't."

"Why not?"

"A teenage son who needs my attention for starters, not to mention crossing business and pleasure. It all makes for bad timing." Her voice dropped to a whisper. "But then, I haven't felt this way about someone since Mike's father."

"You don't talk about him much. I don't even know his name."

She shifted and nestled back against him to avoid looking into his eyes. His hand lightly massaged her arm, but to her it might as well have been a cattle prod against her skin. Her head began to buzz and her heart pounded.

But at the same time, she felt safe in his arms, safe enough to tell him more.

"Randy. His name was Randy." Sadness gripped her heart and she sighed. "We'd been married for three years. Mike was two the last time he saw his father." She pressed her lips together before continuing. "It was an automobile accident on a section of the Interstate in central Arizona that wasn't as built up as it is now."

When her voice dropped to barely a whisper, Marty knew he didn't want her to relive it again for him. "Don't say anything else. I crossed the line. I should have waited until you were ready to tell me on your own."

Stephanie angled herself to him and took a deep breath, "I am ready."

"Only if you're sure."

She gripped his fingers tightly and looked at him. His half-closed lids partially hid his rich brown eyes that were staring at her fingers entwined with his. She waited until he looked back at her face before saying, "I'm sure."

Chapter Twelve

Mike threw his hockey bag down at the foot of the steps once he got home. "Mom!" he shouted. "You here?"

Only silence answered him.

"What has gotten into her?" he asked the face that looked back at him from the small mirror on the wall near the door. "She's acting like . . ." he searched for the right word, ". . . me, when I met Patty." He grabbed the edge of the table and, stiff-armed, leaned forward. The skin around his right eye was turning a shadowy shade of purplish black. No wonder it hurt so much.

He walked into the kitchen and tore open the freezer compartment of the refrigerator. Fumbling around inside, he located a package of frozen broccoli and held it to his eye as he walked up the stairs and to his room.

"Like mother, like son," he said right before he slammed the door.

* * *

Stephanie angled herself on the sofa in Marty's office and laid her elbow on the backrest. She rested her temple on her fingertips. Marty sat next to her.

"Randy was driving back from Phoenix very late at night. I told him to stay there and come back in the morning, but he said he didn't want to be away from Mike and me any longer than necessary." She felt tears glisten in the corners of her eyes. "It's only a two-hour drive to where we lived, and . . ." Marty reached for her, but she stopped him with a wave of her free hand. "And I really wanted him home too." She looked down at her lap. A single tear trailed down her cheek.

"What happen?" Marty urged in a low voice.

She wiped the tear from her face with the back of her hand. "No one knows really. The next morning, a state trooper noticed skid marks. Randy's car had gone off the side of a small mountain on the Interstate. By the time someone got to him, it was too late." She took a long, deep breath. "He'd been gone for a while."

Stephanie felt a shiver in reaction to her own words. She could barely think straight and didn't realize Marty had taken her into his arms until she melted into his chest. As he held her, she felt safe, and the carefully controlled tears she had been fighting finally ran free.

"Shh," he calmed, "it's all right. Go ahead and cry." He rocked her gently back and forth. "It's all right."

She tried to concentrate on the soothing tone of his voice, but the memory of that day in Arizona broke through. She pushed him away. "No, it's not all right. I fell asleep. It's all my fault."

"Stephanie, from what you told me, it was no one's fault."

"Yes, it was. Don't you understand? I fell asleep. I didn't notice he was late because I was sleeping. I could have called someone. Someone might have been able to find him in the ravine in time and make a difference." She looked at him, feeling a full range of emotion dance across her face. She saw him blanch slightly and, for a moment, look away. "Now you know." Her voice quivered. "It will be my nightmare for as long as I live."

Marty's face tensed. "I know all about nightmares, honey, and this one you need to share." His unsmiling lips barely moved when he spoke. "Stephanie, look at me." His hand moved to her cheek for emphasis and their eyes locked. "Don't do this to yourself anymore."

Her lips opened and she wet them. Her chest rose in a deep breath as though she didn't know what to say. His hand left her cheek and brushed the hair beside her ear.

"Have you ever allowed yourself to believe there was nothing you could have done to change what happened?" he pressed.

Stephanie's eyelids became half-shuttered when she dropped her gaze. Marty's fingertips pressed up on her chin forcing her to look directly at him.

"No," she whispered.

"Then do it now."

This close to her, he could see every color in her eyes. A single unconscious blink came quickly and comprehension rushed across her face. He saw her begin to relax and then smile sadly. Eyes glistening, she tried to shift her gaze to the ceiling, but he gently cupped her cheek and wouldn't let her.

"It's okay to grieve. Maybe even for twelve years. But it isn't okay to punish yourself by shutting everyone else out."

"Don't make me do this." Stephanie sniffled and looked into his eyes.

"You have to."

He could see her shaking and the urge to hold her was overwhelming, but he didn't think he'd be able to stand it if she pushed him away again. "Let me help you."

"Why would you want to help me?"

The tremble in her voice was nearly his undoing, but he held on. "Because I care about you, Stephanie. If you need a more complicated answer, I've never met anyone like you."

"You have met hundreds, thousands, of people by being a sports star. Of course you've met people like me," she countered.

Marty frowned. "What are you saying?"

Stephanie sieved her hand through her hair. "I'm just an average person, a single mother trying to do the best for her son. I have no real time for anything except Mike and my job." She hesitated. "And I'm not sure I want to change things right now."

Marty was taken aback by her statement. The silence between them was almost lethal until he finally spoke. "Yes, I've met thousands of people because of who I am, but you're different." He turned fully to face her. "You are by no means average or ordinary." His thumb massaged the back of her hand as he continued. "You're an intelligent, beautiful woman, who cares about family and values. You're down-to-earth, focused, a great mother, committed to making sure your son has a good start as he prepares to face his future. These are wonderful qualities."

She flashed him a wary glance. "We're out of sync, you and I. You're used to attention and being in the spotlight. I'd rather avoid something like that, especially now at this important time in Mike's life."

"Stephanie, you're not listening to me," he interrupted. "I told you earlier that you were perfect and I meant it." He put his hands on both sides of her face and brushed the hair behind her ears.

"Marty, your impression of me—"

"Shh. Let me finish. Okay, you and I are different, I concede that, but I don't see a problem. I see adventures."

Stephanie stood up, stunned by what he was saying. The urge to reach out and hold him was tearing her heart apart.

"Ever since I met you, I've had this weird feeling that I'm finally living my real life. Before you, it was nice, and I thought I had everything, but now, being with you, it seems rather disingenuous." He stood up and pulled her into the safety of his arms and kissed the top of her head. "But this, you, Mike, everything, is genuine and much better."

"So . . ." she said, pulling in a jerky sigh.

Silence hovered between them.

"So, I suppose you don't want to go out on a real date with me and see where it leads, do you?"

"A real date?"

"Yes. No pretend business meetings or brochure drops. Dinner. A movie. Dancing. A planned and agreed upon date." He smiled. Not the careful, tentative smile he saved for pauses in conversation or for people he didn't know, but a real smile that came from the heart.

She said nothing for a long time. She said she would make a decision and this was as good a time as any to do it. She pulled back and squared her shoulders.

"Maybe I could use a little adventure too. You can teach me which fork to use when there are six next to my plate and I can show you how to make a grilled cheese sandwich using toast and a microwave. But I do have to warn you about something."

"Is it going to involve any type of frozen vegetables?"

She laughed. "No. If I do go to this party with you, I don't feel comfortable having to buy a dress that would cost me more than it would cost to send Mike to college for a semester."

Marty laughed with her. "In silk, in jeans, in a flour sack, it doesn't matter to me what you wear, as long as you wear it with me. You're perfect just the way you are." His smile beamed. *And someone I think I could love.*

It was well past eleven when Stephanie got back home. She saw Mike's hockey bag on the floor next to the wall and tossed her keys on the table. "Michael, I'm home," she called up to the second floor. Music fell down the staircase as she saw him open the door to his bedroom and then quickly close it again. Must have lost the game, she thought.

She clicked on the light next to the sofa and sat down, wanting to soak in everything that had happened in the last few hours. Just thinking about it made her heart swell and her blood race. She felt so comfortable with Marty, easily sharing her feelings and her fears like she never had with anyone before.

And now she also felt free, like a giant weight had been lifted from her shoulders. Her body warmed as more tension flowed out of it when she thought back to the way Marty had made her feel safe in his arms.

Mike's music again filled the air. She put both hands on the sofa cushion and stiff-armed herself to standing. She would savor the feeling once more after saying her ritual good-nights to Mike.

Once at the top of the stairs, she put her hand onto the doorknob to Mike's room and knocked lightly. "Mike, do you need anything? I'm going to bed now." Only silence answered and she furrowed her brow. She knocked again. "Mike, is everything all right?"

"Sure. Fine." The closed door muffled his reply.

Almost immediately, she knew something was wrong. She and Mike always made a point of talking to each other before they went to bed, and not through closed doors.

She turned the knob and the door easily opened. "Mike?"

His back faced her. At the sound of her voice, he turned. Her eyes widened as he tossed her the bag of broccoli he had been holding over his eye. She caught it, dropped it, and strode over to him all in one motion.

"What on earth happened to you?"

Mike looked her squarely in the eyes and shrugged his answer. "I guess you could call it a locker room adjustment."

Stephanie folded a well-worn blue washcloth over a few ice cubes. This was not good, she thought. She was about to have a life-altering conversation with her son and she wasn't prepared for it at all.

"Sit," she instructed, pointing to the chair nearest the sink once Mike joined her in the kitchen. She handed the wrap to him. "Hold this over your eye for a while."

"I've been using the broccoli since I got home an hour or so ago. It's not going to get much better," Mike said.

Stephanie brushed the light brown hair away from his face. "What happened?" she calmly asked.

Mike removed the washcloth from his eye and tossed it into the sink. The ice cubes broke free from their confinement and rattled around before settling. "I told you, I had a little disagreement in the locker room."

"I can see that, but I sense there's a little more to it than you're willing to volunteer right now."

Mike looked at her and then let his gaze settle onto the wooden tabletop.

"We might as well get things out into the open," she suggested. "We've never had secrets between us, and now isn't the time to start." She paused. Mike hadn't moved. "I probably need to go first." She pulled in a deep breath. "There's something I'd like to tell you, something about me and Marty."

"I already know," Mike contended, setting his mouth into a straight line that could not be mistaken for anything but disapproval.

Mike's body language shouted betrayed. Stephanie slid out a chair and sat down facing him. "What do you think you know?"

He folded his arms across his chest. "I know that you and Mr. St. Claire are getting pretty tight."

"I guess we are. That's what I want to talk to you about."

He shifted in the chair and interlaced his fingers behind his head. Slouching, he made sure his eyes held hers. "He already did."

"What are you talking about?"

"St. Claire asked me all about you when I got to the rink before my game."

Stephanie felt the muscle next to her right eye start to

twitch. She massaged it into stillness with her fingertips. "What do you mean he asked all about me?"

Mike straightened. "He asked my permission to date you."

"He did?"

"Yep."

"What did you say?"

"I said no."

Stephanie nodded. "I see."

He snorted. "I saw you on the practice rink with him. Joey saw it too. I bet my whole team saw it, and if they didn't, Joey will make sure they at least hear about it."

"Mike, I'm sorry that Joey is being a pain, I really am. I know how hard kids are on each other."

"I got blindsided. It's just been you and me. You should have said something."

Stephanie reached out and touched his hand. "Yes, you're right. I probably should have. But Mike, if I had, I don't think it would have changed anything; not the way I feel and not the way you do." She felt him flinch and held his hand a little tighter. "And I can tell you this for sure, anything that may happen between Marty and me will never change the bond we have and will always have."

Mike looked at her for a long moment. "I have a test tomorrow. I have to study."

His voice seemed less angry, "Michael, we still need to talk about this," Stephanie cautioned.

He stood. "Later, okay?"

Chapter Thirteen

" Aaahhhhh!"

The scream made Tina come running into Stephanie's office. She still held the morning's mail in her hand. She saw Stephanie at her desk, head on the At-A-Glance calendar on the desktop, right arm extended. She dropped the envelopes and ran to Stephanie's side.

Tina shook her by the shoulders and Stephanie raised her head a little. Tina's voice was uneven when she spoke. "What's wrong? Do you need a doctor?"

"Not an MD," Stephanie replied, waving her outstretched hand. She lifted her head more fully. "Maybe a psychologist, though." She sat up. "I'm a head case today."

Tina visibly relaxed. "You scared the heck out of me," Tina grumbled, smacking Stephanie on the arm before sitting down in the only other chair in the room. "I thought you had a heart attack or something."

"You could say that," Stephanie agreed.

Tina kicked at the mail on the floor until it was in a

pile before bending down and picking it up. "I haven't heard you shriek like that since the day you found a mouse in the cabinet under the sink in the ladies room."

"This is much worse than a mouse."

"Apparently." Tina laid the mail on the edge of Stephanie's desk. She picked up a stack of books piled near the telephone. "Do these have something to do with that scream a minute ago? *Teens and a Single Parent, Coping with Adolescence.*" She pulled out a two-inch-thick hardcover and rolled her eyes, "*The Parent Alone.* I think you need the Cliff Notes on this one. What's going on?"

Stephanie leaned back and sighed. "Michael."

"Did he take the car again?"

"That, I could handle. He's a little upset with me because I didn't tell him I was seeing Marty."

"You didn't tell *me* you were seeing Marty. When did this happen?"

"I'm not seeing him, per say. It's more like I'm beginning to see him. Sort of. Maybe."

"If this is how you told Mike, then I can see why he is upset."

"That's the trouble. I didn't tell him. Apparently he saw Marty kissing me at the ice rink."

Tina held up her hand. "Whoa, girl. You were kissing Marty again. And at the ice rink no less. When?"

"Last night. But that's not the issue."

"You sure kiss him a lot for someone who kinda, sorta thinks."

"I know, I know. I screwed up. Mike somehow got into a fight with one of his friends about it."

Tina crossed her arms over her chest. "I think I agree with Mike on this one. You should have told him."

"I didn't know something was going to happen until last night."

Tina waved away the comment with a swipe of hand. "Of course you did. With all the kissing going on, how could you not?"

Stephanie slid her elbows onto the desktop and dropped her head into her hands. Guilt plucked at her and tightened its fist around her stomach. "You're right. I should have mentioned to Mike that I might, possibly, perhaps, on the outside chance there could be a slight attraction, maybe think about exploring the option of getting to know Marty on a personal level."

"Whew," Tina replied, "You tap-danced all around that rather nicely."

Stephanie closed her eyes briefly. "I didn't know anything was going to happen, so how could I discuss anything? Suppose I was totally wrong? I'd feel like a fool."

"Stop making excuses," Tina scoffed. "Anyone in the room can feel the electricity flowing between you and Marty when you're together. It was only a matter of time. You should have hedged your bets and clued Mike in." She flipped a hand in the air. "Teens and raging emotions can be really complicated."

Stephanie swallowed the lump that was forming in her throat. "I let him down, didn't I?"

"I don't think you let him down. I think he just feels a little betrayed that you let someone else into your life and didn't check with him." Tina uncrossed her arms. "Not that you have to check with him, mind you. It's only been the two of you for so long. Throwing someone else into the mix probably feels weird to him."

Stephanie sighed. "You're right. He said no anyway."

Tina held up her hands in a defensive posture. "Wait a minute. I thought you told me you didn't talk to Mike."

"I didn't, but Marty did."

"For two people who kiss so much, you don't seem to be able to stay on the same page for long."

Stephanie slapped the top of her desk. "And there it is. Now you know why I'm so confused."

"You should have dated more and gotten some practice so when Mr. Right finally skated into your life, you'd know what to do."

"I suppose I should talk to them both."

Tina nodded. "But that will have to wait a while."

"Why?"

Tina stood. "You have the soft grand opening of the new Sporting Goods store at the mall with Marty and the reception afterward."

Stephanie smacked her forehead with the heel of her hand. "The reception for all the local bigwigs who helped develop that former landfill site. I did forget. Maybe I can beg off."

"Not in your life," Tina countered. "Coreman will have your head if you try. The St. Claire account is important and so is snagging the PR contract for the new store. It's a national chain with mucho potential. He needs the deal and you need the exposure. You'll have to go."

Stephanie slouched in the chair. "I seem to keep stepping into bigger and bigger holes, don't I?"

"Everyone makes mistakes."

"But mine are whoppers. I let my emotions get the best of me. I fantasized a relationship with a famous, hunky sports star, put my job on the line and, worst of all, let down my son."

"You didn't let him down. Stop saying that. You just have poor timing. And that's something that can be corrected with practice."

Stephanie nodded and felt faintly ill. She had the feeling that timing was going to be the least of her worries.

Mike's reflection just over her shoulder in the hall mirror startled her. She finished adjusting her earring and slowly turned to face him.

"You look nice, Mom," he simply said.

"Thanks." She adjusted her black suit jacket, stalling for a little more time, knowing this might be her chance to bring up Marty again. "The new Sporting Goods store is opening tomorrow. Tonight is the reception for everyone who worked on the project."

"St. Claire going to be there?"

Stephanie nodded. "He's doing a PR stop. The store is carrying a heavy line of hockey equipment. The Coreman Group represents both Marty and the store, so it's a good opportunity for me."

"Ah-huh."

Stephanie's shoulders dropped. "Mike, what do you want me to do?"

"Do you like him?"

Stephanie looked deep into her son's hazel eyes. Not a boy anymore, but not anywhere near a man, Mike hovered in that complex stage of life between dependence and individuality where truth was important and trust could be broken in an instant.

"I like him very much."

Mike didn't react.

"Is that a problem?" she asked.

"I don't know."

"Do you want to talk about it?"

He shrugged. "You're going to be late."

"I can be late."

A car horn sounded and Mike turned toward the door briefly before turning back to face his mother. He looked at his watch. "That's Trey. He's early. He's taking me and Joey to practice."

"Joey?" She put her thumb and forefinger under his chin and angled his face to the light. "The Joey who is responsible for the multicolored skin around your eye?"

He nodded. "We came to an understanding. He's going to keep his nose out of our business and I'll keep my fist away from his face."

Stephanie laughed and took his hand in hers. She looked down, realizing her fingers barely closed around it. Her heart skipped back to a time when his entire hand fit into the palm of her own. It seemed like forever ago. When she looked back into his eyes, he smiled.

"Later, Mom," he said, kissing her on the cheek before grabbing the hockey sticks next to the door. He put his hand on the doorknob and then stopped. He turned slowly. "Have a good time."

As the door closed behind him, Stephanie admitted that, like it or not, time moved forward. Children grew up. Situations changed. Her fall on the ice had set into motion circumstances that could very well alter her life and Mike's, and she didn't think she wanted to stop any of it.

"How are you? Nice to meet you."

The attendees moved through the reception line like candy on a conveyor belt, Marty graciously shaking everyone's hand as though each was an old friend. From across the room, Stephanie sipped some sparkling water and admired his poise and patience.

"Your man looks good," Tina said, stopping to join her on the way to the buffet table.

"He's not my man," Stephanie countered.

"Couldn't tell that by the way he keeps looking over here at you."

"He's probably just waiting for the signal to sit down. He's been standing there meeting and greeting for about an hour now."

Tina glanced at her watch. "He's got about five more minutes of personality duty. What do you say we go in and find a seat?"

As she walked into the dining room with Tina, Stephanie felt like a disappointed schoolgirl and then like a woman scorned when she realized she had been ex- pecting to sit next to Marty at this affair. But this wasn't an official dinner, just an informal gathering of busi- nessmen and local representatives. Marty would have a place at a reserved table with the organizers and owners. She would have to scramble for a seat at an empty table like most of the attendees. Another reminder of the dif- ference between them.

She and Tina found a seat at a back table and made small talk with their dinner mates. Stephanie watched for Marty out of the corner of her eye. Her breath caught when she saw him enter the room, and was pleased when he scanned the area until he found her. His smile grew wider when his gaze locked with hers.

She felt herself warm as she watched him walk to his place at the head table. He looked at her over the rim of his glass and sipped the water inside. She felt a blush move over her cheeks. As he talked with the members of his dinner party, he often glanced in her direction and seemed delighted when she acknowledged him with a smile.

"And you haven't heard a word I said."

Tina's words made Stephanie turn toward her. "I have so." She reached for her water glass and took a healthy drink, all the while trying desperately to imagine what Tina had been saying to her. She put the glass back down on the white linen tablecloth. "Okay. You win. I wasn't listening."

"Too busy ogling your hockey hunk."

"I wasn't ogling. He is my client and I want to be sure he isn't too bored here."

Tina nearly spit out the buttered roll she had just taken a bite of. "Bored!" she exclaimed. Stephanie gave her a withering look and she dropped her voice. "That man's positively world-weary from trying to keep a smile on his face. You're going to owe him big time."

Stephanie was about to offer an argument when the owner of Sporting Goods tapped a spoon on his water glass and began the formality of announcements. She directed Tina's attention to the head table with a waggle of her finger. Then she pasted on her brightest smile and pretended to be interested.

Through the clatter of silverware, Stephanie barely listened to the obligatory thank-you speeches and promotion announcements. Her ears perked up, along with most of the female senses in her body when Marty was introduced.

She listened to him thank the owners for inviting him, his rich baritone voice cutting into her, affecting her like the reverberating vibrato of a tuning fork. She closed her eyes and let the tones envelop her right up until the time she felt an elbow in her side.

"Hey, you look like you're having a rather pleasant dream," Tina cautioned. "Try to be interested."

Stephanie's smile beamed. "Believe me, I am."

"Good work, Stephanie," Roger Coreman said as they left the reception. "I see a lot of prospects for this deal. Let's go over a few tomorrow about ten."

"I'll be there, sir," Stephanie replied. Coreman nodded his acknowledgement and left with his wife.

Stephanie began to leave when she felt a hand on her elbow. "I'd like to go over a few prospects now."

Smiling, she faced Marty. "Don't tell me. I know. I owe you for this."

"I began doing a lot of these grand openings when I was a rookie and continued through the first few years of my career. After a while I promised myself I'd never do another," Marty said, gently steering her toward his car. "They can be a bit painful."

"Unexciting, huh?"

"No, I don't mind that part. People are quite interesting, actually." He rubbed his eyes with his thumb and finger. "Flash bulbs are hard on the eyes." He looked at her. "Right now, you're a silver circle with hair."

"Some compliment."

"As soon as I get my eyesight back, I'll correct that." He opened the passenger car door. "Want to grab some coffee? I haven't really seen you all night."

"I'll have to tell Tina that I won't be needing a ride home first," Stephanie said as she slid into the seat.

"No need. I already told her," Marty replied with a wink.

Chapter Fourteen

Stephanie sat at one of the tables in the outdoor café and waited for Marty to bring their drinks. A brisk summer breeze whipped the scent of good coffee into the air and lifted the hair from her shoulders. She tilted her head and enjoyed the feeling. When she opened her eyes, Marty sat opposite her, staring.

"I didn't hear you come back. How long have you been there?" she asked reaching for the paper cup.

"Not long." He smiled.

Stephanie removed the lid and raised the cup to her lips. She looked at him over the rim as she sipped. "Good cappuccino." She took another sip and set the cup down on the tabletop. "Thanks again for doing the opening."

"I probably should do more. I made a few good contacts, and some of the businesses are going to explore the possibility of advertising on the boards at the rink. The Sporting Goods store, for sure." He raised his paper cup in a salute. "And I have you to thank for that. If everything works out the way I hope, I won't have to increase the cost of ice time, and all the teams will be able to afford to keep playing at the arena."

"Mike would be devastated if he couldn't play hockey."

Martin's shoulders suddenly slumped and he sat back in his chair. "I think I may have caused a little problem with Mike."

She rested her arms on the table and leaned forward. "How so?"

"I think I stepped over a line I shouldn't have crossed."

"Oh?"

Marty pressed his lips together before speaking. "I asked him how he would feel if we dated."

"He told me."

"He did?"

"We don't have many secrets between us, and the small ones teenagers think they do usually come out rather quickly."

"He didn't seem to like the idea much," Marty continued.

"There's a little more to it than that. Apparently some of his teammates saw us kissing in the back rink and gave Mike the business about it."

Marty shifted uneasily in the metal chair, his knee hitting the table leg, making the coffee shake in the cups.

"Should I talk to them?" Marty offered.

Stephanie waved her hands frantically in front of her face. "No. Bringing any more attention to Mike will only give the guys another reason to rag on him. It'll work itself out."

"You're sure?"

"Everything works itself out, Marty."

He looked past her and then looked back into her eyes. "Do you think he could get used to the idea of us seeing each other on a regular basis?" he asked, testing her reaction.

A slow smile curled her mouth. "Maybe."

"Could you?"

"I see some possibilities."

"I wouldn't want to put a wedge between you and your son."

Stephanie's face became serious. "No one could ever do that. It's been just the two of us for so long that the bond we formed is unbreakable." She relaxed her expression in response to the caution she saw in Marty's eyes. "But the bond does shake every now and then with no real damage done." She noticed that his eyes hadn't left her face. "Are you all right?"

"Yes."

"Do I have some dirt on my nose or something?"

"No, why?"

"You're looking at me rather oddly."

Marty gave his head a quick shake as the breeze began again. "Can I be perfectly honest?"

Stephanie grimaced. "As long as it doesn't hurt."

"You fascinate me."

"I do?" The words came out like a denial.

"You have since the first day we met."

Stephanie laughed. "A memorable occasion. Me on a stretcher, you running alongside it."

He leaned closer to her and took her hand. "That's not what I meant." He reached out and brushed the hair from her eyes. "How do you feel about me, Stephanie?"

She closed her eyes a moment, let out a long breath and opened them again. "I like being with you."

"That's all?"

She pressed her lips together and furrowed her brow as if in thought. "I guess you can say I'm very flattered, Marty."

He let her hand go and sat back. "Flattered?"

"You're an incredibly attractive man. And look around." Taking in a steadying breath, she did just that, scanning the tables filled around them. "Beautiful women everywhere. Most of them looking at us, at you really. I'm very flattered that you picked me."

"That's still not an answer to my question."

With her lip caught between her teeth, she tried to think of a better answer for him. With a sigh, she sat back. "Marty, I have a lot to sort out in my life. It could take a lot of time."

"What does taking time have to do with a man and a woman caring about each other?"

"You care about me?"

He stood, took her hand and pulled her to standing. He nestled her body into his. "Yes, I care about you." He looked at the hand on his arm, the delicate fingers, the soft skin. "I want to see where a relationship with you can lead. I know you need some time, more time than we've had together so far. But I've waited a long time to find the right woman, and I think I may have. I don't intend to make a temporary commitment if you don't feel the same way."

"I might. I mean, I could. Maybe." She couldn't form a coherent sentence for some reason. His serious gaze grew too intense for her and she shut her eyes against the hopeful look that crossed his face.

"Stephanie, look at me."

She opened her eyes again.

"I don't want you to say or do anything that you feel is wrong for you. I can wait." He smiled. Her lips parted, a hint of tears sparkled in the corners of her eyes. His hand brushed her hair again. "Tell me how to make you happy."

She dropped her gaze. His knuckles pressed up on her chin, forcing her eyes open to confront his gaze.

"Just be with me," she whispered.

He pulled her closer to him. She didn't relax, but she didn't resist. When her body nestled closer to his, she reveled in the way they seemed to fit together.

"I intend to do just that." He pressed his lips to her forehead and then kissed her temple. She lifted her chin and they kissed with an intensity that sealed the pact they had just made.

When he lifted his head, she became aware of a rhythmic sound around them. As her practical senses returned one by one she realized the people sitting around them were clapping. She buried her head in his chest and laughed.

Marty nodded to acknowledge the attention. He pulled out a few bills from his pocket and dropped them onto the café table. He kissed her on the top of her head. "I think I should take you home."

They drove back in his car and parked it in the middle of her driveway. Marty angled toward her in the seat. "Now what?"

Caution moved into every part of Stephanie's body. She had a wonderful time tonight with Marty, but she had some loose ends with which to deal. Mike among the most important. With everything that had happened, everything that had been said, the evening was going to end here outside her home.

She hoped her voice wouldn't betray her prudence when she spoke. "I had a great time." She leaned forward and looked up through the windshield. "Mike's light is on, so he's home. I should be going in." She tossed her head to lighten the tone she set. "Don't want him to think I'm making out with you in a car in our driveway. What kind of example would that set?" She glanced out again.

Marty studied her upraised face bathed in moonlight. He could smell her perfume. "We haven't scheduled our date yet."

"Wasn't the Coffee Café a real date?"

"Hardly. But there's a cocktail party at my house on Friday. I'd like you to come."

A date. A real date. Now that he'd asked, she questioned the wisdom, or lack of, accepting. "A big cocktail party?"

"Not so big. About twenty or so people. The magazine that did the photo shoot there is actually hosting. It's a wrapup event for everyone who worked on the spread."

Stephanie slid back toward the car door. "Can't we start with something smaller and less conspicuous like a movie?"

"We could," he conceded, "but I'd really like you to be at the party with me. As my date, my for-everyone-to-see date."

Stephanie bit down on her bottom lip. "Tuxes and big-deal evenings gowns, I suppose."

"Black tie, but a causal black tie," he reassured. "How formal can twenty people get around a pool?"

She stilled. Could she make that huge leap of faith? Was she ready to hand her heart completely over to a man like him and trust him not to smash it into a gazillion pieces after all these years of carefully guarding it herself? Wishing she could see into the future, she said nothing and stared out the windshield.

She'd been so careful to always do the right thing for so long, but without risk there had been little chance of growth. Mike was fifteen now. Maturing and changing like crazy. In a few years, he'd be off to college, leaving her, as he should, to do some growing of his own. If she was ever going to take a chance, it had to be now.

As if feeling her thoughts, Marty took her hand, gently pulling her closer to him. Reaching out he wound his fingers in her hair and closed his mouth down on hers. Stephanie placed a hand on his shoulder and kissed him back.

"I told you, I can wait." His voice was low but tender. "But try not to make me wait too long."

"Okay." She blinked up at him.

"Please try to trust me. I would never hurt you," he said.

"Okay," she said again.

"So I can send a car for you on Friday then?" Marty asked.

"I don't feel all that comfortable in sequins and imported lace."

"Then wear jeans and a T-shirt. Just be with me."

"I don't know."

Marty leaned over and kissed the tip of her nose. "How about we leave it at this—I'll send the car. You have up until the time the driver gets to the estate to decide if you want to."

"And it'll be all right with you either way?"

"I'd rather have you with me, but I'll respect your decision."

She was about ninety percent sure he'd have a better

time at the party without her, and offered him an alternative that hardly eased her conscience. "I tell you what, if I decide not to go, I promise that the next time you ask me to go somewhere, I won't refuse." She suffered the weight of guilt as he kissed her again.

"Agreed. But I can hope."

She slid out of the car and watched him back out of the driveway. She followed the red tails lights of his Porsche until they disappeared around the corner. As she walked to the front door, she looked up at Mike's bedroom window. She definitely needed to talk to him.

She walked through the front door, dropped her keys on the small table against the wall and headed for the kitchen. Mike had his head inside the refrigerator and she could hear him sliding some bottles around on the metal shelves inside it.

"Hey," she said when he closed the door and turned around. "I thought you were in bed."

Mike had a quart of milk in his hand and headed for the cabinet next to the microwave. "I got hungry." He poured milk into a glass.

Stephanie reached into the cookie jar and took out a few chocolate chip cookies. She handed them to him. "These should help."

He waited until he drank half of the milk before he took them from her. "Have a good time?" he asked, sliding a chair out from under the table.

"Yes." She motioned to the other chair. "Mind if I join you for a while?" Mike shrugged his answer and she sat down.

"Sure."

She tossed her head toward the backyard. "I saw a whole mound of stuff piled near the trash cans."

"I worked on the basement today. Part of my at-home community service, remember?"

Stephanie smiled. "Not easy to forget why you have to do it."

"I'll get the garage done this weekend. Then, if I am correct, I have about three weeks of grounding left before you parole me."

Her smile broadened. "Want some help with the garage?"

"No," Mike said with a quick shake of his head. "I screwed up, so I'll fix it. Everything always seems like a good idea at the time."

"Did for me when I was fifteen." She glanced down at her hands briefly before looking back at her son. "Are you real tired, or can we talk for a minute? I really need to talk to you about Marty."

"I figured it was coming sometime."

"It won't be so bad, I promise."

"Do you like working with Marty at the rink?"

"I liked it better when he was just the coach."

"But you love hockey, and I would think you'd like one of your favorite players taking an interest in you."

Mike sighed. "Mom, there's a kind of pecking order you don't understand."

"Tell me."

"It would be nice to get attention from someone who played in the pros, but I'd rather it be for my ability, not because my mom's a hottie."

Stephanie smiled. "I didn't think I was a hottie."

"Aw, Mom, you know what I mean." Mike clasped his hands together and rolled his thumbs. "It just feels weird."

She reached over and put her hand over his to stop

his nervous gesture and let him know she was going to be serious. "We need to come to some sort of compromise."

Mike nodded. "I know. Been thinking about it."

"I'd like to get to know Marty better, and I can't unless I spend some time with him." She saw a look of anxiety flash in Mike's eyes and quickly reacted to it. "But I promise, I'll always be there for you. It won't matter how old you are, where you live, or anything. I'll always be there for you."

Mike looked down at the floor for a long moment. "I know that too," he said looking back at her face. "I guess I just needed to hear it again."

Chapter Fifteen

The next day Tina dropped the morning's mail on Stephanie's desk. "I hear your Prince Charming is having a little get-together Friday night. So are you going to the ball?"

"It isn't a ball, it's a cocktail party," Stephanie countered as she scooped up the envelopes and sifted through them. She picked out one that didn't look like a bill and opened it. "And I'm not sure if I'm going yet."

"Of course you are," Tina said firmly. "This is a great opportunity to show the world that the man's taken. A man like that won't be alone long if you decide to throw him back."

"Tina, you don't understand."

"I do, honey. I understand perfectly." Tina rounded the desk and touched Stephanie on the shoulder. "Want to talk about it?"

Stephanie looked at her pessimistically. "I'm a little scared."

"Tell me why you feel like that."

"Marty makes me feel wonderful."

"That's a good thing."

"But he may be out of my league."

"That's nonsense, and it's apparent he doesn't think so."

"I think he's being kind."

"A man like him doesn't have to be *kind* in that manner," Tina pointed out while circling the desk to sit down.

Stephanie shrugged a reluctant agreement. "He did say that he cared about me and wanted to see me a lot more."

Tina pressed her hands on the desk and leaned forward. "And what did you say?"

Stephanie bit down on her bottom lip. "I said okay."

Tina dropped back into the chair rubbing her head. "A totally gorgeous hunk of male humanity told you that he cared for you, and all you said was okay?"

"He took me by surprise." The stunned look on Tina's face made her uneasy. "I should have said something else, right?"

"Hello. One of the most eligible men in the universe told you that he wants to spend more time with you. That's a *real* good thing." Tina grabbed the phone from its cradle. "Call him and tell him you'll be there on Friday."

Stephanie grabbed the phone from Tina's hand and replaced it. "I can't do that."

"You're right," Tina agreed, "calling from the office isn't romantic." She reached over and shut off the notebook computer on the desk. "Go over there and tell him in person." She raised her eyebrows up and down. "Then you can kiss him again. Like, seal the pact."

"I can't do that either." Stephanie held up the letter she'd opened earlier. "I have to go down to the Food Mart and get a signature on this representation contract." She retrieved her purse from the bottom desk drawer and stood. "I talked them into a two-year deal."

"Okay, maybe it isn't so bad. After you get the signature, go next door to Footsteps and get some new shoes." She looked down at Stephanie's black pumps. "You can't go to a fancy ball in sensible shoes. You need some sexy sandals."

"I'm still avoiding reaching that conclusion."

Tina waved off the indecision. "You're going. Get very strappy ones," she called out as Stephanie headed down the stairs. "Black. Not shiny. Maybe satin. And oh," she continued shouting as Stephanie walked down the stairs, "no stockings with those sandals! Get a pedicure!" She raced to the edge of the staircase and yelled down. "Red polish! Red is sexy!"

Stephanie waved but never turned around. Sure, she could get shoes and a pedicure, but what else was she supposed to wear. The only thing she had other than a few business suits was a horrible powder-blue dress she wore when she was a bridesmaid in her cousin's wedding.

She should probably just stay home.

Michael yanked open the back door to the Coreman Group's offices and took the steps two at a time. "Yo, Mom!" he called out. "You here?"

Tina stepped out of her office. "Hey, Mikey, heard you did a little dancing with your friend, Joey."

"Hey Aunt Tina," Mike said placing a kiss on her

cheek when he reached her. He looked around. "My mom here?"

"She just left."

Mike's shoulders dropped. "Oh."

Tina held his chin in her hand and angled it to the light. "So, who won?"

"It was a draw."

"I bet." She walked back inside her office and motioned for Mike to join her. "Your mom should be back in an hour or so. Want to wait or can I help you?"

Mike nodded thoughtfully. "Maybe. I was going to talk to mom about something, but it might be better this way. Can you get some time off?"

"Now?"

"Right now. It's important."

"You weren't driving again, were you?"

"No, nothing like that. C'mon. I need your expertise. Can you get off work?"

"I suppose." Tina reacted to the intense look on Mike's face. "Is everything all right?"

"Yeah. Mom and I had a little talk last night and a few of the things she said got me thinking." He heaved a sigh. "I can't expect her to sit home and wait for me to decide what I want so she can get on with what she wants."

"Doublespeak, Mike," Tina challenged. "Say what you mean."

"She should date someone."

"Someone?"

"Okay, maybe she should date Mr. St. Claire."

"Why the change of heart?" Tina saw the faintest bit of red color Mike's cheeks right before he smiled.

"Because she smiles more since she met him."

"I agree, but you should be telling her, not me."

Mike grinned. "I have a better idea."

Stephanie always thought that Gordon's Gourmet Emporium looked more like a mall than a supermarket. A two-story sprawling building with greenhouse windows across the front on the second floor and three outdoor cafes at ground level, as well as a restaurant that served some of the exotic food imported for sale, it catered to those with a more exotic palate than she had.

She'd only been inside Gordon's once, when Emeril appeared to sign his latest cookbook and share a few cooking secrets with those who were willing to pay for a gourmet cooking lesson that the store was hosting after the book signing. With unique programs like that and other special events such as wine tasting and chef de haute cuisine, representing this exclusive store would generate a healthy commission for her with writing press releases alone.

She scanned the parking lot as she walked to her old Mustang. There were enough Mercedes', BMWs, and Audis parked in front of the store to make it look as though she was walking into a luxury car show. She stashed her briefcase with the coveted signed contract inside in the back seat of her car when Marty's Porsche pulled into the space next to hers.

"Hey, pretty lady."

She closed the back car door and turned, watching him ease his toned body out of his car. "I didn't expect to see you here."

"I came to pick up some lunch. Care to join me?"

She wrinkled her nose. "I never developed a taste for

caviar and Brie." She put a hand to her stomach. "I've finely honed my body on burgers and fries."

Marty let his gaze slowly drop to her ankles and then rise even more slowly back to her face. "And a fine job you did."

"Cut that out." She gave him a playful whack on his arm. "I'm here on business. I just signed Gordon's to a two-year PR deal."

"Congrats," Marty said, lightly taking her arm and steering her toward the building. "Let's celebrate."

She stopped him. "I'd rather not eat here."

Marty looked at the diners filling up the padded seats in one of the outdoor cafes. "You're right. Too crowded. Wait here. I have an idea."

Tina pulled her car into an empty space right in front of Bloomingdale's. "Okay, Mike. We're here."

Mike reached into the back seat and retrieved his backpack. He pulled out a magazine with the corners turned down on some of the pages. He put it on his lap and put both hands on the cover. "I feel bad about giving my mom such a hard time about seeing Mr. St. Claire." He lowered his eyes. "I guess it's been the two of us for so long that I didn't want to share her."

Tina reached out and touched Mike's cheek. "Aw, that's sweet. But a little selfish. You'll be off to college in a few years, partying with babes, pledging fraternities." She flicked his nose with a finger. "What do you want your mom to do, sit home and wait for you to bring home the laundry?"

"Ow." Mike's eyes watered and he rubbed the tip of his nose. "I know, I know. Anyway, I want to make it up to her." He picked up the magazine and began to page through it.

Tina snatched it from his hand. "*Elle*. Very nice." She handed it back to him. "Show me."

"I think she should go to that party on Friday night and I think she should wear this." He folded the cover of the magazine under and handed it to Tina. "And I want to buy it for her. She's always getting me stuff. I want to return the favor *and* tell her to go out and have a good time."

She looked from the pages to Mike a few times without speaking. "Mike, this is beautiful, but do you know how much it costs?"

He shook his head.

"It's Versace. It's expensive."

"I've been saving the money from my part-time job at the ice rink. How much?"

"A lot more than we both have to spend on a dress."

"How much?" Mike repeated, his eyes downcast, looking at the beautiful dress on the beautiful model on the glossy page. He looked back at Tina. "I really want her to have something like this."

Tina looked at Mike's hopeful face. "I may not be a fairy godmother, but I think I know what we can do."

Marty spread a checkered tablecloth across the wooden picnic table near a lake about two miles from the store. Sunshine filtered through the leaves of the maple tree shading them, striking Stephanie's hair, giving even more life to the highlights surrounding her face. The breeze picked up, catching the strands in a playful dance.

Stephanie brushed the hair from her eyes and helped

Marty unpack the rest of the basket. "You bought all this at Gordon's?" she asked.

"Right down to the tablecloth."

"I'm impressed."

"Good. That's what I was going for." Warmth and amusement flashed in his eyes. "Hope you're hungry." He set out two bone china plates and silverware before producing two wine glasses and finishing the table setting.

Stephanie skimmed her hand around the rim of the glass. "Actually, I am." She watched him dole out equal servings of marinated asparagus and seasoned chicken topped with a scoop of small golden balls she wasn't familiar with. She poked at it with her fork. "What is this?"

"It's Amur River Golden Ossetra Caviar. It's a Siberian delicacy."

Stephanie wrinkled her nose involuntarily. "No matter what you call it, it's still fish eggs."

"Come on, give it a try." He put a flat pancake on her plate. "Put some on one of these."

"And that is?"

"A Russian pancake called blini." He reached into the basket and brought out a container. "Put on a dollop of this creme fraiche and I assure you, you'll like it."

"Now it looks . . . fattening."

"It is, but I'm counting on you still loving me even if I gain twenty extra pounds."

Stephanie gathered enough confidence to comment, "Who says I love you now?"

Marty didn't say anything. He just looked at her, a slow smile curving his mouth, making her want to smack his arm. But how could she smack him just for knowing the truth?

"You do," he quickly answered. "It's in your eyes, your smile, and the way you kiss me." He took out two baguettes of French bread and slipped one onto her plate. "One of these days you're actually going to have to say it out loud." He grinned. "I just hope I won't need a hearing aid to hear it."

Stephanie picked it up and took a bite, allowing herself some time to both appreciate the taste and to think. "Okay," was the only word that she could muster into uttering.

"You told me that once already. I would like to hear something a little more definite."

She watched him finish chewing the bread he'd been sampling and wash it down with a long swig of sparkling water. Just as he plunked the green bottle down on the tablecloth, she heard Tina's voice inside her head screaming, *"Tell him already."*

"I know I feel something, something special," she whispered. She looked away and then looked back. "I'm a little afraid."

"I would never do anything to hurt you."

"I know that." Her pulse began to race. Her fingers traced the shape of his face, feeling the muscles in his cheek jump with her touch. "It's hard to explain."

"Do you think I'm using you somehow?" he asked after a few stunned seconds of silence.

Stephanie's heart seemed to have climbed into her throat and stalled there as she looked into his eyes. "No. Darn. I knew I wouldn't say it right." Nervously, she shifted, trying to find a place on the ground that was a bit more comfortable. But it was her own words that had made her edgy. "If anything, I could be using you to make a better life for Mike and me. We may be attracted to each other, but we don't fit together very well. Our lifestyles are so opposite. Even you have to admit that."

Marty braced himself and pulled her close. "Here's what I'll admit."

The kiss came at her like a bird of prey, smooth and powerful. But also with precise communication of how wrong her assumption has been. Gentle reassuring hands kneaded her shoulders. His palms then ran down her arms in a smooth caress. He never stopped kissing her, never lost the connection, as he pulled her to standing with him, responding to her doubt with tenderness and loving warmth.

Blood pounded in her body in a blinding roar, blocking out all thoughts except that of the man in her arms. It was darn hard not to believe him. She had to think, but couldn't. Not when he was kissing her like this. She jerked back her head and pulled her mouth free of his. "Marty, do you know what I was doing today before I got here?"

"Something tells me that no matter how I answer you, it's going to be wrong, so tell me."

"I was figuring out my commissions for the month. Adding up how many bills I could pay and how much I could buy because of your signing with the agency. That isn't exactly romantic."

She saw something in those gorgeous eyes of his that made her heart nearly stop beating. Fear? Dread? It couldn't be understanding. How could he possibly understand living paycheck to paycheck when he was worth millions? They were right back at square one: Unwilling to acknowledge that each needed the other for totally different reasons, maybe none of them love.

"All right," Marty said, his tone edgy. "You want honesty? You'll get honesty. I promise that I will never give you anything less."

Stephanie tried to swallow the lump that was in her throat as she agreed with a nod.

"I think that we met for a purpose. I think you're ready to get on with your life. You're over the horrible fate that your husband met, and you need me to prove it to you."

"That could be true, but I think you deserve a princess, someone to jet around the world with and share champagne and caviar." She looked over at the food he bought for her. "I can't eat stuff like that. It isn't me."

"Wrong. Dead wrong," Marty said without an iota of doubt in his voice. "You make it sound like I'm a material person without a soul."

"No, that's not it. I think you might be happier with someone, well, elegant."

He reached out and with infinite care, outlined her chin with his finger before running it across her lips. "You're more than elegant. You're a timeless classic." He wound his arms around her and splayed his hands across her back. "You center me, Stephanie. You make me remember what's important in life. And I want you around me forever so I never forget."

She swallowed, stared up at the clouds above them and then back at him. "I'm afraid that you'll get tired of a routine life with routine responsibilities and commonplace dinners. Maybe you're attracted to me because I'm a change from the fast-paced world you live in?" She saw the light in his eyes fade with her words.

"You think I'm shallow enough to toy with a woman's heart like that?"

She saw his shoulders suddenly hunch, the expression on his face change to one of concern. "No, no," she said quickly.

"You think I only care about you because you're a change from the norm for me? Not only are you wrong, but you're also being unfair. Don't judge me by the persona I needed to present sometimes to survive in the public eye. Judge me on how I am inside."

She saw a shard of frustration cut through his eyes. "I swear that's not what I meant." She let out a breath, struggled with a few words and then began again. "Over the years I came to realize that men don't really want a ready-made family in suburbia. And that's all right. I understand."

"Not all men," he countered. "When I first met you after you fell on the ice, I admit I didn't think of you in terms of a relationship. But I also have to admit, I felt something right from the start. Then we spent time together. Talking time. Laughing time. Professional and personal time. I got to know all aspects of you and I like each and every one of them. I like them so much that I can't imagine not being with you."

"Maybe."

"There is no maybe. I'm not saying that being successful doesn't help in a lot of ways, but as key as success is, what we have and can have in the future is much more important than just enjoying the perks." He kissed her gently. "Please trust me. I'll make sure that you feel safe no matter where we are. I promise you that."

Her heart began to pound against the wall of her chest. Her worst fear had been that she would embarrass him somehow, that she wasn't in his league. But the honesty in his eyes told her that he had meant everything he had just said. She tried to speak, but the words wouldn't form.

Marty pulled her close. "Honey, we can take it as slow as you need to, but I can't be friends with you any longer. I want more. Come to the cocktail party with me. Let me show you how good we can fit together no matter where we are."

Stephanie looked into his incredible eyes and saw a sincerity that was her undoing. "Okay."

Chapter Sixteen

Tina and Mike pulled up in front of a stone-front building with large windows outlined in small white lights.
Mannequins dressed in beautiful gowns of silk, geor-
gette, and chiffon posed inside.

"What is this place?" Mike asked, getting out of the
car and slamming the door. He circled around the front
of Tina's car and looked up and down the elegant street.
The sidewalks were cobblestone. Old world-type street-
lights dotted the spotlessly clean streets with tall, lush
green trees lining the roadway, making it look like a
postcard picture from a town in Europe.

Tina locked her car with a remote chime and put her
arm around Mike's shoulders. "This, sugar pie, is down-
town in the Hills."

Mike looked around as a silver BMW passed, followed by a Jaguar and then a Cadillac. "Nice place, but
what are we doing here?"

Tina stepped forward and opened the door to a store
called Encore. "Realistically, a fairy godmother isn't go-

ing to show up and give your mother a beautiful gown to wear to the ball, but I bet we can find just the right one in here." She swept her hand in an inviting arc and ushered Mike in.

Inside the store mirrored its stylish surroundings outside. A few chairs with clawed feet and tapestry seat cushions sat near large full-length mirrors. Two red velvet love seats formed a seating area in the center of the room. A glass counter near the back also served as a case for jewelry in an illumination of lights which showed off their brilliance. But the only dresses in view were those in the window.

Mike turned a small circle on the woven woolen Oriental rug. "There's nothing here. And I really don't think any of the ones in the window are mom's type." He stopped his circle when he came back to face Tina. "Besides, this looks expensive."

Tina patted Mike's shoulder. "Relax, honey. This store, Encore, is where the socialites of the Hills bring their 'can-only-be-seen-in-once' dresses after some mucky muck event. Encore then re-sells the dresses at a fraction of the cost and donates the proceeds to a charity chosen by the person who brought it in. We can get a twelve-hundred-dollar dress for about two hundred dollars. It's a can't-lose situation."

Mike raised his hands, palms up, in a questioning pose. "What stuff?"

At about the same time, a woman with white hair stylishly wound into a bun and dressed in a perfectly fitting black silk suit came out from behind the heavy green brocade curtains at the back. "Welcome to Encore. How can I help you?"

Tina walked forward, hand extended. "We need a little assistance with a transformation, and you look like just the woman who can make it happen."

Mike pulled Tina aside. "Aunt Tina, I don't have two hundred dollars."

Tina smiled. "No problem, I owe your mom a birthday present." She turned to the proprietor. "Bring out your best. We've got some shopping to do."

Stephanie knelt in front of her closet tossing shoes over her shoulder. "I should have listened to Tina," she groaned as a brown clog flew over her shoulder and hit the dresser. "I have nothing in here." She got onto her hands and knees and burrowed to the back of the closet. "This only proves I should stay home tonight." She was still tossing shoes over her shoulder when she heard the front door open and close.

"Mom, where are you?" Mike called out from the living room.

"Up here!" Stephanie shouted.

Mike ran up the stairs, taking them at his usual two at a time. He leaned the white box tied with a red ribbon on the wall outside his mother's bedroom before going inside. Once there, he was assaulted by the sight of shoes and clothes strewn all over. He could barely see the bed and he couldn't see his mom at all.

"Mom! Quit kidding around. You don't have time to play hide and seek with me."

"I'm looking for shoes," a muffled voice returned.

"Where?"

"In here." Stephanie backed out of her closet and stood. She held a pair of black pumps in one hand. "These are the best I can do." She plowed through a pile of dresses on the bed and picked up the blue cocktail dress she'd worn to her friend Janet's wedding. She looked into the mirror on her dresser and held the dress in front of her. "I shouldn't go," she said, dropping down onto the pile of clothes laying across the bed.

"Yes, you should," Mike replied.

Stephanie stood and hung the dress in the closet. "I feel like there are a hundred butterfly wings banging against my stomach and I'm still in the cocoon."

"I think I can solve that." Mike walked to the bedroom door and shouted, "Aunt Tina, come up now!"

"What's Tina doing here?"

Tina strode into the room with a huge black satchel slung over her shoulder. "I'm going to help make you even more beautiful than you already are." She looked around the room. "What happened here? Target practice for tanks? The place looks like it exploded."

"No, but that wouldn't be a bad idea," Stephanie replied. She started to hang some clothes back in the closet. "I was looking for something to wear and failed." She spun to face her son and her friend. "I don't think I'm going out tonight."

"After what we went through this afternoon, you most certainly are, missy." Tina responded to the confusion on Stephanie's face with a swipe of her hand. "Michael, show your mother what's behind door number one."

Mike ran into the hallway and came back with the white box he'd hidden there. He held it out. "This is for you from me and Aunt Tina."

Stephanie looked from her son's face to Tina's. Smug satisfaction danced across both. "What have you done?" she asked, sitting on the bed and putting the box down next to her.

"Mom, I want you to go to Mr. St. Claire's party tonight. I want you to have fun." Mike leaned over and gave her a kiss on the cheek. "And I don't want you to worry about what I think, because I think you probably should have done fun things like this long before now."

"Are you sure?"

"Yes, very," Mike replied. "Now open the box."

Stephanie smiled and ran her hand across the white box and onto the satin ribbon. "What's in here?"

Tina stepped forward. "If you don't open it, you'll never know *and* you'll be late."

The ribbon opened easily with one tug. Slowly she opened the box and pulled back the pink tissue paper. She stared at the contents for a moment before looking up with the sparkling eyes of tears she was trying to hold back.

"This is a Donna Karan," she said, fingering the tag. "How can we afford this?"

"Tina knows of this special shop, and I saved my money from my job at the rink," Mike replied.

"But a lot of the time you were working off the community service. How did you . . ."

Tina reached down and retrieved the black dress inside and thrust it into Stephanie's hand. "Oh for the love of Pete, we'll have time for sentiment and explanations later. Get dressed and let me finish you up."

The dark fabric slid over Stephanie's hand like liquid. For a moment, she hesitated putting it on, afraid that she'd somehow tear it. But when she did, she felt as though she had been surrounded in a soft cloud.

The dress wrapped around her as though it had been made for her. It fell from the heart-shaped bodice in a delicate line, hugging her body and accenting her curvy figure. She turned in a small circle and marveled how the fabric seemed to flow and ebb like a moonlight tide caresses the shore.

"Silk chiffon," Tina said with a nod. "Stop trying to pull up the sleeves," she said, smacking Stephanie's hand away from the material. "It's an off-the-shoulder style."

"You look great Mom," Mike said, satisfaction glowing on his face.

Stephanie put her arms around him and held him close. "I can hardly believe you did this for me."

"Okay, break it up," Tina said retrieving the satchel she'd placed on the floor. "We're not done here." She set the bag on the bed and rummaged through it.

"I feel like I'm dreaming," Stephanie said, looking at herself in the mirror. She turned to Tina. "If you pull out a magic wand, I don't think it would surprise me at this point,"

Tina held up a makeup bag and a can of hair spray. "Not a wand, but magic nonetheless. Sit. The dress is perfect, but now we have to do something with the rest of you."

"I'm done," Tina announced as a final spritz of hair spray hissed in the air. "What do you think?" She moved so Stephanie could see herself in the bedroom mirror.

"I think that's not me." Stephanie raised a hand and touched her shoulder-length hair, now stylishly tousled. "How did you do this?"

"Spray and Scrunch," Tina replied. "What do you think Mike?"

Mike's smile lit up the room. "I think my mom looks like a princess going to the ball."

Chapter Seventeen

The car carrying Stephanie stopped at the apex of the driveway arc at Marty's front door. Extra floodlights illuminated the area, but were hardly necessary because of the thousands of tiny white lights outlining almost every tree outside the house. Fresh flowers had been planted in the meticulously groomed flower beds and white-jacketed attendants waited to lead the guests through the front door and to the party.

The car door opened, but Stephanie did not move. Her frayed nerves seemed to have frozen her solid to the seat. The driver reached his hand to her as the muted sound of a female voice singing filled the air. "Miss?"

Stephanie placed her hand on the one offered and stepped out of the car. Almost immediately another white-coated attendant was at her side.

"This way, please," he said, bending his elbow and offering his arm.

She smiled and accepted the escort. "Where will you be?" she asked the limousine driver as she walked away.

159

"Mr. St. Claire said I was yours for the evening. I'll be there with the other drivers." He pointed to a long line of cars to the left.

Feeling more at ease, she took the attendant's arm and walked with him to the front door. There, another white-jacket man greeted her. "The other guests are in the back garden."

Stephanie nodded and began a slow walk toward the source of the lovely voice she could hear singing. The large French doors leading outside again were open and she paused. Taking a deep breath, she stepped into what could only be described as a wonderland.

The mellow baritone voice came from the lead singer of a five-piece ensemble performing on a temporary wooden stage. A dance floor had been placed in a large area to her right where a dozen or so couples moved gracefully to the beat of the pop tune. A buffet seemed to go on for miles and several waiters walked unceasingly among the partygoers offering to fulfill their every need.

She turned to the sound of popping corks signaling another round of champagne being served, and that's when Marty saw her. For what felt like an eternity, they did nothing but look at each other, seemingly frozen in time.

Marty drew his gaze away from her just long enough to put his glass down on the tray of a passing waiter. Her breath came faster as he approached her. He was perfection. His tuxedo fit him like molded ebony marble. His eyes, like a strong electromagnet, held hers and would not let go. With each step he took closer, her pulse rate soared.

When he reached her, he leaned forward, a muscle

throbbing in his jaw. He moved his mouth to her ear and whispered, "I've been waiting for you." He kissed her cheek and took her hands. Stepping back an arm's length from her, his gaze swept her head to toe. "You look . . . incredible." He led her to a small empty table and pulled out one chair. "I was afraid you wouldn't come."

"I almost didn't," she admitted, sitting. She waved off a glass of champagne offered to her by a waiter who seemed to appear from out of nowhere.

Marty mimicked her gesture and sat down across from her. He took her hand across the table. "Now the party is complete."

She drew her gaze from his eyes and looked around. She had never seen anything like this. The tone of the social gathering amazed her. Everyone seemed to know each other well enough to be content to see and be seen until someone stepped from the house to join the gathering. Then necks craned and voices merged, laughter echoed and the music wove it all together.

She returned her attention to Marty. "There are so many famous people here." She glanced to her right. "Isn't that Senator Chambers and his wife talking to Ron David from the Mets?"

Marty glanced over his shoulder. "Yes. Ron has been rehabbing with the Trenton Thunder and he was just cleared to return to the Mets. He was kind enough to join the fundraiser. Do you want me to introduce you?"

Stephanie waved off the offer. "No, thanks."

"Yankees fan?"

She smiled her answer and watched as photographers snapped candid pictures while guests jockeyed for position next to one luminary or another. "Is this what you do on weekends?"

"Only once in a while."

A very feminine hand suddenly fell on Marty's shoulder. Stephanie followed its contour to bare shoulders, a plunging neckline, and the instantly recognizable face of Kaylee McReynolds, obscured for the moment by a half-empty crystal glass. Stephanie smiled in acknowledgment, but the smile quickly faded when none returned.

"Martin. Wonderful party, as usual," Kaylee said, lowering the fluted glass and leaning down and shifting so that her red evening dress became even more alluring. She kissed him on the cheek. "You make me wait this long to see you? Shameful."

Marty rose. "Kaylee. You remember Stephanie."

"Yes. We met briefly at the photo shoot." Kaylee set her glass down on the table and stepped closer, appearing to dissect what she could see of Stephanie from head to toe. Her brow furrowed for a moment and then smoothed as a grin arched her lips. "Lovely dress."

"Thank you."

Kaylee began pulling Marty with her. "You will excuse us for a moment, won't you, darling?"

Marty pulled away. "Can we do this later?"

"Actually, no." She took a small step backward and peered at Stephanie. "You can bear a few minutes alone, can't you?"

"Of course," Stephanie stammered.

"I'll make this quick," Marty promised as Kaylee led him away.

Sitting alone, Stephanie struggled not to feel conspicuous. A few people acknowledged her with bland smiles but otherwise did not engage her in any type of conversation. She sipped her sparkling water and looked around. To pass the time, she counted the somebodies she could recognize. The collection of local public figures and names from almost every entertainment and sports venue was pretty impressive.

The band moved into a slow song and a few couples began to dance. Others, who had been on the dance floor moving to the pervious more upbeat tempo, moved to make room. The change in ambience allowed Stephanie a chance to leave the table in a natural flow of bodies. When she turned, she ran right into Marty.

"Sorry. I still have no idea what Kaylee really wanted. She rambled on about charities and shops." He moved closer to her and slipped his arm wound her shoulders. "I'm sure she had a point, but I couldn't find one. I couldn't wait to get back to you." He picked up her hand and kissed her knuckles. "I am so glad you're here."

"So am I. This is incredible." Around her lightbulbs flashed, people laughed. Everyone seemed to be having a wonderful time.

"Like the music?" Marty asked.

She nodded.

"Let's dance." He took her hand and led her to the dance floor, snaking his way around people and returning comments with a smile or a nod.

As she walked with him, panic descended upon her. Her palms went sweaty and her eyes grew huge. She had never been much of a dancer. "I'm not sure this is a good idea," she said as they reached the edge of the wooden floor set down over the grass. "I've lost count of the number of men I've probably crippled by stepping on their toes."

"You'll be fine. Just hold me like you mean it," he said, leveling her arms around his neck.

His face was close and the music filled her head. She

felt as though she had been thrust into a furnace. She
nestled her cheek more deeply against his and found she
couldn't breathe, couldn't think straight when she felt
the beginnings of a beard nuzzle her jaw. She closed her
eyes, swayed against him and sighed. They seemed to
move almost magically together through the dancers. He
felt good in her arms, too good.

"Here comes my patented move," Marty said, suddenly spinning her out and then pulling her back into his
arms with a casual grace. He laughed as her eyes widened, and drew her back as close to him as he could.
"What do you think?"

Her hands braced his shoulders. Lights spun around
them and the music soothed. Just as she relaxed, he
whipped her out again, spun her in two quick circles and
pulled her back. She saw his eyes light with delight when
she laughed.

She caught her breath when her body hit his. "You've
been practicing."

"Honey, I've had to dance with more people than you
could ever imagine." He gently kissed her cheek. "But I
never wanted to do it more than now."

She reacted by missing a step, hitting solidly into what
she thought must be a wooden bar. She turned in time
to see a waiter trying to steady the two fluted crystal
glasses that were on his tray. He grabbed one before it
fell, but the second hit the rim and splashed its contents
to the floor.

Right at Kaylee's feet.

"This is a three-thousand-dollar dress!" Kaylee
shrieked, taking two steps backward when the champagne hit her shoes.

Stephanie felt her stomach sink—of all the times and

all the people, she lamented silently. She swiped at Kaylee's dress with her hand. "I am so sorry. Did any get on you?"

Kaylee pushed Stephanie's hand away. "Lucky for you, no."

"Nothing's ruined," Marty assured. "It was an accident."

Kaylee looked down at her feet and then glared up at Stephanie. "These shoes are Prada. They're wet and ruined." She began to move toward Stephanie when Marty stepped between them.

"Don't cause a scene, Kaylee. There are more important things in life than your shoes. Wipe them off. They'll be fine." Believing no other explanations were necessary, he put his arm around Stephanie and walked away.

Stephanie looked briefly over her shoulder. Kaylee's face was an angry shade of red, and her eyes warned as their gaze locked. Stephanie made a mental note to stay as far away from her as possible for the duration of the party.

"Just ignore her," Marty said leading Stephanie to a quiet spot. "She's like a diva. Beautiful, talented, but very wrapped up in herself."

"You and she were an item once, weren't you?"

Marty blew out a breath. "Once."

She watched his face cloud with an emotion she could not immediately identify. "Touchy period, huh? I shouldn't have asked."

"Under the circumstances, it's actually a fair question. We liked each other well enough for a while, I guess."

"It seems like she's not quite over you."

"Well, I'm over her." He kept his eyes on hers. "I got

caught up in the spotlight and everything that went with it when I met Kaylee. After a few months I realized she was all show and no heart." He tapped his chest with his fingertips. "I need heart if I'm going to commit to someone." He traced her cheek with the same fingertips. "Someone like you."

She touched his arm. "You deserve better."

"There is no one better." He looked at the hand on his arm and lifted it. "You need a ring on that finger. Maybe someday you'll let me give you one."

She moved back and pulled her hand from his. "You hardly know me."

"I think I do." He stepped forward and touched his lips to hers.

Panic came again, but not the same kind she'd felt before. She was kissing Marty at his own party in front of everyone and wondered if they would care. Then came a feeling of contentment that bubbled inside her and burst through, forcing her surrender. She put her hands on his shoulders and kissed him back until the sounds that had blurred around her became clear again. As the music and voices rose once again in her ears, she stepped back and looked around. Everyone seemed to be looking back.

"I need to . . . powder my nose." She broke away from his gentle grasp and moved quickly through the crowd into the house. She saw him begin to follow her and was glad when he was cut off by a few of the guests trying to engage him in conversation.

Needing to think, she hurried into an ornate powder room on the first floor. She put her palms on a marble countertop, leaned forward and took a deep claming breath. When she looked up, the mirror told her that she wasn't alone.

Kaylee had stopped primping a few feet away from her and was staring. Stephanie studied the angry expression on the beautiful woman's face in the mirror and she felt her heartbeat rise, this time in dismay.

"If you came in here to try to talk me into letting Marty go without a fight, you may as well turn around and leave," Kaylee said, stepping closer.

"I'm not going anywhere," Stephanie replied, hoping her voice did not betray her uneasiness.

"Good." Kaylee put her black sequined purse on the countertop. She walked to Stephanie and took her arm in a gesture that shouted control. "Because you and I have to get something straight. Marty's going through a phase right now. He thinks he wants to be average, but trust me, I know him, and he doesn't. He's going to get over this interlude and he's going to be sorry." Her disapproving gaze raked over Stephanie. "It was a bad idea for you to come here tonight."

Stephanie wrenched her arm free. "I have as much right to be here as you do."

"You think so?" Kaylee tipped back her head and laughed. "Did you see the people out there? The crème de la crème of society. Where do you think you fit with them? He needs to be with someone who can relate. He needs to be with me. He'll come to realize it soon enough."

"Marty was right about you," Stephanie said, her anger clearly showing. "You *are* a snob."

Kaylee crossed her arms over her chest and cocked her hip. She looked Stephanie up and down. "Tell you what. I'll let you continue to play with him tonight," she said, arrogance coloring her voice. "Stay here in your last season's dress." She glanced down at Stephanie's feet. "And your black plastic shoes." She picked up her purse and put her finger under Stephanie's chin. "Stay and indulge your fantasy. It doesn't matter. You'll still be a pumpkin after midnight."

Before Stephanie could respond, she turned and walked out, leaving Stephanie alone to mull over Kaylee's parting words.

Marty checked his watch again. It had been far too long since Stephanie left him. He moved through the crowd, carefully searching for her, stopping near the edge of the pool to scan the area one more time before going into the house.

Kaylee came up behind him and arched an arm around his neck. "Looking for your little friend? I think she's on her way home."

Marty could see the satisfaction of settling scores in Kaylee's eyes. "What do you mean she's going home?"

"We were chatting in the powder room and I quietly pointed out a few fashion faux pas she had made. I'm afraid she didn't take it very well."

Marty removed her arm. "Kaylee, you don't do anything quietly." He glanced over her shoulder.

Kaylee put her hands on his waist to stop him from leaving. "I may not have been as tactful as I could have. Don't be angry with me. I'm only looking out for your best interests."

Marty stepped back beyond her reach. "What did you do?"

Kaylee batted her eyelashes brazenly. "I simply told her the truth and pointed out that maybe she was in over her head coming here. After all, this isn't a party for the help." She stepped forward, one hand on his chest, the other around his neck. "We could be so good together again."

Marty peeled her from him. "It's been over between us for a while now, Kaylee." He held her wrists to keep her from throwing her arms around him again. "I think you know that."

Kaylee yanked herself free. "I know that it's only a matter of time before you come to your senses and realize that we belong together."

"I came to my senses about you a long time ago."

A ruckus made them turn to their left. Stephanie had bumped into a chair and knocked it over. When she tried to pick it up, so did a waiter and they knocked heads. With hand gestures, the waiter seemed to assure her that he could handle the situation. Stephanie grimaced her apology.

Eyes blazing, face tight, she rubbed her throbbing scalp with her fingertips as she approached. "We didn't finish talking," she said to Kaylee in a controlled voice. She glanced at Marty. "Girl talk." A nervous smile faded as quickly as it appeared.

"Oh we were quite through," Kaylee replied smugly. She grabbed Marty's arm in a death grip. "You can run along now."

Stephanie's eyes widened. She reached out and wrenched Kaylee's hand free. "No, *you* can run along."

"Marty, your newest little project has spunk." Kaylee turned her gaze to Marty. "But you should have taught her manners."

"I have manners," Stephanie said, her tone irritated, "what I don't have is a nose so high up in the air that I could drown when it rains."

"Well, I never heard anything so rude!" Kaylee shouted back.

"If you're going to continue to talk down to me like I'm a hired hand, you had better get used to it."

Kaylee turned and placed her hands to her hips. "Martin, are you going to let her talk to me like that?"

"Yes, actually, I am." Marty was grinning from ear to ear. "It's not that I like cat-fights, but Stephanie is doing a great job of telling you what a lot of us have been trying to tell you for a while now. You should listen to her."

Kaylee's face registered pure shock. An instinctive movement caused her to step back. When she did, she ran out of ground and fell backward into the pool. The accompanying splash sprayed water on Marty and a few revelers standing nearby.

Kaylee emerged, her platinum hair plastered to her face, streaks of eye makeup running down her cheeks, and spit out a mouth full of water in a most unladylike fashion. Thrashing around, her hands kept breaking the surface of the water flinging droplets on those coming to help her. When she managed to get to the edge of the pool, there was enough fire in her eyes to dry everyone who had gotten wet.

"Get me out of here," she demanded, hanging onto the tiled edge with one hand and reaching out to Marty with the other.

A crowd began to gather. Each person who gravitated poolside put more distance between Stephanie and Marty. Stephanie tried to wave to him but several people blocked his sight line. She tried again, but soon realized there was no way she was getting near Marty as long as Kaylee was commanding the attention.

Soon, a few of the local reporters sent to cover the event elbowed their way to the front of the crowd and began to take pictures. Through the tangled rumble of the voices, she could hear words like "society page story" and "jealous cat-fight." She saw one reporter begin to look around as people filled him in on their version of what happened.

Before he could get to her, Stephanie dashed around the house to the driveway. The one thing her PR firm, any PR firm for that matter, didn't need was adverse publicity. She'd talk to Marty in the morning, but right now she needed to leave.

Never looking back, she located her driver, jerked open the car door, and lunged into the safety of the back seat. "Get this thing moving," she said quickly, looking over her shoulder and through the rear windshield. "No one's coming. We can make a clean getaway."

The driver slid into place behind the steering wheel. "Is everything all right, miss?"

Stephanie hunkered down below the windows. "That depends if you're the fish or the fisherman."

Marty grabbed Kaylee's wrist with one hand and her upper arm with the other. In one clean tug, she burst from the pool.

"Look at me!" she shrieked, swiping the hair from her eyes. "My dress is ruined, my makeup's ruined!" She paused when she noticed photographers frantically snapping pictures. "I'll sue if any of those pictures get printed!" she screamed to them.

"Calm down," Marty said, taking off his tuxedo jacket and draping it across her shoulders. "You'll probably get a call to do the SI swimsuit issue now." He led her to a chair and sat her down as attendants rushed to get her some towels.

"I knew something like this would happen if you invited someone like her," she said, wringing water from an edge of her dress.

"What exactly is 'someone like her?' " Marty asked, his voice tight.

"You know, ordinary, not at all savvy about the important things."

Marty laughed at her shallowness. "Kaylee, you have an inflated sense of self and have no idea about what's really important."

"And you do?"

"Yes, for the first time in a while, I think I do," Marty said, making sure he held her gaze so she would not misunderstand what he was about to say. "I love Stephanie. I know that I want to spend the rest of my life with her." He signaled to one of the waiters. "Danny, make sure Ms. McReynolds gets something dry to wear. Then call her a cab and wait with her until it comes."

"Get me a cab?" Kaylee repeated in shock.

"Yes," Marty said as he turned to leave. "I'm going to get Stephanie and I want you gone before I get back."

"Surely you don't mean that," she purred.

Marty took two strides back to her. "I have never been more serious in my life."

The long black car pulled into Stephanie's driveway. Once more the driver helped her out. "Are you sure about this, miss?" he asked. "We can get back to the party in about twenty minutes. No one need ever know that you've left."

Stephanie felt a nervous smile cross her face. "Oh, they know all right."

"Are you sure?"

"I'll be fine. Thank you for everything."

She waited outside until she saw the taillights of the limo fade from sight. For some reason, she wasn't angry anymore. Kaylee had actually done her a favor by pointing out the differences in her life and Marty's. As she walked toward her house, she almost felt grateful.

She reached the front steps and suddenly stumbled, catching the heel of her left shoe between the two slabs of her cracked, cement walkway. When she steadied herself, she noticed that the heel had broken from the shoe.

She took both shoes off and held them up in the yellow-tinted porch light. She couldn't help but laugh out loud. "No wonder the heel broke. They *are* plastic."

Still laughing, she tossed them over her shoulder and toward the driveway and climbed the two steps to her house.

Chapter Eighteen

Stephanie sat on the couch in her living room. She plopped her feet on the ottoman and looked at them, wiggling her toes and laughing.

"Donna Karan and plastic shoes. What a combo."

She kicked the ottoman out of the way and leaned forward. She grabbed her ankle and massaged the stiffness she felt there.

"I should have worn my sneakers."

She hit her knees with her palms, got up, and retrieved her sneakers from next to the beanbag chair Mike had salvaged from a garage sale. After donning both and tying exaggerated bows, she danced around the room.

"Oh, you didn't see this in *Cosmo*?" She threw a hand to her chest and blinked her eyes a few times. "Latest trend, you know. All the rage in Europe."

She continued to spin until she felt giddy. Only then did she fall onto the sofa and break into a combination of short giggles and long belly laughter.

"Mom, what on earth?"

Stephanie looked up. When she saw Mike, she let herself fall over into the sofa cushions and tried to smoother her giggles in a throw pillow.

He walked over to her and, hands on hips, gave her a stern look. "What's going on? Is the party over already?"

"Whew," Stephanie uttered as her laughter began to subside. "You could say that." She straightened.

"Did you have a good time?"

Stephanie thought back to the look on Kaylee's face as she hit the water. "You could say that too," she sputtered before breaking up with laughter again. She leaned back, held her sides, and roared. Tears of laughter ran down her cheeks.

Mike gestured like he was pushing down against an unseen force. "You are out of control. I'm going to bed. Tell me about it in the morning."

She tried to compose herself. " 'Kay," she managed to get out before giggling. "Sweet dreams."

Walking into the kitchen, she wondered if Marty would be furious with her. She started to laugh again when she remembered how Kaylee looked in the pool; mouth open, hands flaying in the air, wet hair plastered to her head. Stephanie knew the situation required some kind of commentary. With all the flash bulbs popping right after the splash, a picture was bound to show up on the pages of one newspaper or another.

She wrenched open the refrigerator and drank the milk right from the carton. "No fancy crystal goblets for me," she said before wiping her mouth with her fingers and replacing the carton on the self. "Straight from the cardboard. That's how people of *my* standing drink it."

As she walked back into the living room her mood shifted from buoyant to annoyed. She should have gone with her gut instinct and stayed home. She always shied away from lavish gatherings, political get-togthers and social must-bes. Eliza Doolittle she wasn't. Not her. The rain in Spain leaked mostly in her attic.

She was a grown woman capable of most anything except being someone she wasn't. She'd managed to get this far on her own and she didn't need a Prince Charming swooping down, sweeping her off her feet and changing her life forever. She could . . .

She hesitated. Or did she?

He did make her feel special when he was around. She knew the highs and lows of her life very well, and there had simply been more highs since she met him. It wasn't that she was lonely and wanted to grab on to the first person that showed her some attention. Getting attention was easy. She snorted in a most unladylike fashion when she remembered how all eyes turned toward her right after Kaylee hit the water. Not exactly the kind of attention she would want on a regular basis, but the people at the party had definitely noticed her.

But she wanted more, she had to admit. She wanted love. She wanted to fall into a never-look-back, mad, passionate relationship, but she'd been adrift for years now, avoiding relationships, maybe even being afraid of them.

Now she might have shipwrecked any chance she had of having one with Marty. She'd been a fool not to admit that she cared madly about him when he asked her to do it. And now it just might be too late.

The engine of Marty's Porsche purred to a stop as he turned off the key in the driveway of the small Cape Cod he'd come to know so well. He got out and looked at the front of Stephanie's house. The light was on in the living room. She was still awake.

He slammed the car door and strode up the walk. Halfway to the door, he stumbled over something in his path. With a quick sidestep he regained his balance before reaching down and looping a finger through the thin, black strap of Stephanie's shoe. Beside it was the mate, sans the heel, looking as though she had taken all her frustration out on it. Giving the front window a sidelong glance, he felt a smile curl his lips.

He knew just how to show her how much he did care.

Stephanie heard a car door open on her way up the stairs. Retracing her steps, she got to the door and peeked out in time to see Marty coming up the front walk. She turned and leaned against the door. She knew he would be coming to see her, but she hadn't expected it would be this soon.

Ready for battle, she yanked it open before he could knock and spoke before he had the chance. "It was an accident. Somehow she ended up in the water."

"I know," he replied.

She pulled the door open wider. "You may as well come in, but if you think I'm going to apologize for what happened, you're sadly mistaken. I rather enjoyed it." She walked into the living room.

Marty was right on her heels. "So did I."

She spun to face him. "What did you say?"

"I said I enjoyed seeing Kaylee put in her place." His smile bloomed. "Although I didn't know her place was in the water, I rather liked the result."

Stephanie narrowed her eyes. "Did you set this whole thing up?" she asked striding away and then back. "Tossing me into a fancy-schmancy party and then dancing with me like that to distract me before letting me loose on your ex-girlfriend?"

"Dancing with you like how?" he baited.

She tapped a finger on his chest. "You know very well how. Like I was the only one there. Like I was special. Like . . ."

"I loved you," he finished.

Her first reaction was shock, coupled quickly with an urge to apologize. "You what? I don't think I heard you right."

"Is this better?" he asked, taking a step closer, his voice low and husky. "I love you Stephanie."

Stephanie bit her lower lip in nervous anticipation. "It's very nice."

"I'm not here to talk about Kaylee." He reached up and stroked her hair. "I'm here to talk about us."

"Not the working together us, I suppose," she responded with nervous energy in her voice.

"That's a part of it."

Her heart stuttered in her chest and emotion rose to cut off her breath. "I guess you'll be wanting someone new to represent you." She blew out a long breath of air. "Coreman is going to be on the warpath when he finds out I've lost you."

Marty put a hand on her shoulder. She turned into his touch. "You haven't lost me, Stephanie. You'll never lose me. But I did come here for a specific reason." He took her in his arms. "I'm not leaving until you tell me that you love me."

She inhaled sharply and held her breath. The love was there in her heart, begging to be said, but she had to be sure. "Be careful what you wish for," she warned. "I'm just an ordinary single mom with a six-room house and a teenager."

He pulled her closer. "There is nothing ordinary about you, Stephanie Thomas. You are an incredible woman. I'm never quite sure what you're going to do, but I want to spend the rest of my life finding out."

"Are you sure that's what you want?"

He led her to the sofa and they sat down. "I'm sure. I want you. I want to hold hands with you on the living room sofa, watch old movies, and wait to find out how Mike's day was while our dog sleeps on a braided rug."

She looked into his eyes. It surprised and pleased her to see that the emotion mirrored in those incredible brown eyes showed her that he meant every word.

"And what do I get in return?" she teased.

Marty slipped to one knee in front of her. From inside his coat, he pulled out the shoe he'd found in her driveway. "A happily-ever-after, if you'll let me."

He set the shoe down and took her right foot. After slowly undoing the laces, he slipped the sneaker off and picked up the strappy sandal.

"I've been called the Prince of the NHL and I never paid much attention to that moniker until the day I met you. I knew then I had found my princess."

"I'm not a princess."

"Yes, you are, and I'll prove it to you." He cupped her heel with his left hand. "My princess lost her shoe tonight running from the ball." He slipped the sandal on her foot.

Stephanie looked from her foot to his face. Take it, her mind screamed. Take what he was offering her—the future, the happiness, and the love. Don't worry about using the wrong fork at dinner or wearing a used dress to the opera. Whatever would happen, just let it.

She smiled at him. "It does fit. Must be mine then." Marty rose in a flash and pulled her to standing. He stepped toward her but she stepped back and held up a hand. "You need to know a few things about me," she continued.

"I know everything I need to know."

"Let me finish," she said, sighing. "I'm good at my job, a job I don't intend to give up anytime in the fore-seeable future. I have a wonderful son who, sometimes, will have to come before you do. I hate to cook." She looked around the living room. "And I'm messy."

"I'll take it."

She shook her head. "I'm not done. I don't want to live in an eighteen-room house. I don't want to have to clean it. I have a tendency to ride the clutch on cars and burn it out, so your Porsche is as good as toast." She looked down at her dress. "Clothes like this make me nervous because I'm afraid I'll drop food on them and ruin the fabric." Marty started to say something but she silenced him with one hand. "And Mike tells me I snore sometimes."

Marty waited in silence for a few moments before ask-ing, "Is that all?"

Stephanie raised her eyes, appeared to be counting down a list and then said, "Yes. I think so."

He smiled. "Well, I don't need the Porsche. A nice sedan will do. You have a six-room house, mine is eigh-teen, so how about we comprise at twelve and let some-one else clean it? Your job is an asset. You can help me make the rink more profitable by using your PR skills so, eventually, I can sell it and we can spend more time together. I firmly believe kids should always come first when they need to, and we can order takeout. You be messy, I'll clean up. And I don't care if you wear a flour sack, as long as you wear it for me."

"Hmm," she replied. "I guess then that about covers it."

"One more thing. I've been told by every roommate I've ever had in my NHL career that I talk in my sleep." He lifted her chin with his fingers to make sure his eyes held hers and smiled. "Now I'm done except for one thing. I love you very much. I think I fell in love with you from the very first second I saw you lying on the ice at my rink. No other woman has ever made me feel like you do. I never want that feeling to end."

She felt his body go very still and the fingers on her chin tighten ever so slightly. He cocked his head and brought his smile to within a breath of her lips. Then he kissed her with an eagerness that affirmed his dreams and hopes for their future, promised long nights of cuddling on the couch in front of the TV, and growing old together as they met their future.

Emotions poured through her at such a furious pace that she needed to catch her breath. She pulled away and looked into his warm eyes. What she saw there confirmed what she felt in his kiss.

"You asked me to trust you, that you would never hurt me," she whispered. "And I didn't answer you."

"Can you answer me now?"

If she was going to tell him at all, now was the time. "Yes. I do. I was so afraid for a while that you didn't care as much as I did."

"I couldn't love you more." He brushed an unruly lock of hair from her brow, his gaze running over her face as though he could never get enough of her. "You're the one woman who can open up my world and my heart."

She reached up and cupped his cheek. "I do love you Martin St. Claire," she said, touching her lips to his.

"Took you long enough," he replied before taking her in his arms and vowing to never let go.

Epilogue

Stephanie smoothed the skirt of her white silk gown and swept the attached train behind her. The lace sewn over the silk organza of the off-the-shoulder neckline itched a little, but she didn't care. She had just gotten married.

"You look gorgeous," Marty said as the final guest left the church vestibule. "I have never seen a more beautiful bride."

"It's the Vera Wang," Stephanie quipped. She smiled. "Previously worn by the governor's daughter last year and bought for a song at Encore."

Marty laughed and pulled her close. "You amaze me, Mrs. St. Claire." He kissed her, pulling her up into his arms so that her feet dangled in mid-air and one satin shoe slipped from her foot.

"Hey, Cinderella, you lost a shoe!" Mike called out as Marty put Stephanie down.

"That's what started this whole thing," Stephanie said, laughing. She slipped the shoe back on her foot and looked over at her son. Mike had just finished blowing up a vinyl tube about twelve inches long. "What on earth is that thing?"

He held it up for her to see. "Cool, huh? It's called a thunderstix. They come in pairs." He angled one toward her. "Stephanie and Marty. June 25. Romantic, I guess."

"Cute, but what are they for?" she asked.

Mike winked at Marty. "You'll find out soon enough," he said before ducking outside.

"Shouldn't we go out too?" Stephanie asked Marty.

"Let me enjoy my wife alone for a few minutes," he replied. "Once the reception starts, I'll have to share you. It took me two years to convince you to marry me, and then another year for you to actually do it."

Stephanie tapped her forehead with one finger. "Good planning on my part. In three months Mike is off to college and we have the house to ourselves, albeit a rather large twelve-room house."

"So let's fill it. With kids," Marty suggested with a smile.

"You're not serious."

"I am. You did a great job raising Mike. I'm laying down a challenge here. Do you think you can do the same with our kids?"

Stephanie looked at him through narrowed eyelids. "Bring them on!"

Marty's eyes blazed with anticipation. "Can't wait to start."

With that the front door to the church opened and the best man signaled for Marty and Stephanie to come out. They walked out to the waiting limousine through an arch of crossed hockey sticks held by the ushers. The thunderstix roared in the air as the guests hit one against the other in loud approval, just as fans do during a hockey game.

At the curb Stephanie stopped. Tied to the bumper of the car were hockey skates and black strappy sandals. She turned to Marty. "Nice touch."

He grinned. "Just for you. I love you honey."

"And I love you back."

As they got into the car, Stephanie could hardly believe it had all happened. She settled comfortably into the protective arch of Marty's arm and sighed. No one might believe this fairytale began with a fall on the ice, but now there was no doubt in her mind that it was going to end where it should—happily ever after.